The Red Brick Road

Robert P. Wills

Cover illustration by

Milena on Fiverr.com as "MilenaVitorovic"

Cover design by

Rebecca on Fiverr.com as "RebecaCovers"

Copyright 2018

A boy got there first. He went down a different path.

Table of Contents

Chapter 1
Kansas

"Get off my squash!"

The young man ignored the driver as he ran across the top of the vegetable cart. He was honestly trying to not step on the vegetables, but the wagon was completely full of them.

"Dang kids," the driver added as a final admonishment when the youth jumped off the back and ran off.

The youth ducked around another wagon- this one full of much more substantial milk jugs and blocks of cheese- before darting into an alley. He took deep breaths to keep his speed up.

Today it was going to be close.

"Jus' another minute, Sam. Jus' another minute!" The disheveled young man begged in a nasally voice. "Barney'll make it. He always makes it." He looked over his shoulder. "Just take your time and look at the clouds or somethin'. There's lots of them this morning. Havin' a convention or something."

Sam looked down from the loading dock. He wasn't much older than the boys standing before him. Thanks to his size however, he seemed several years older. "You goops think you can tell me what to do?" A smug look on his face. In truth, several of the boys were actually older than him, but it didn't stop him from pushing them around. Partially because of his size, but mainly because his father owned the distributions rights to the paper- the Okaloosa Independent. "You are lucky I even let you sell these papers!"

"Come on, Sam. Y'know Barney sells more pape's than... than anyone."

Nods from most of the other delivery boys as well as several girls, attested to this fact. The hard truth was that since Barney could read, it made it easier for him to scan the paper and tailor his hawking to individual customers as he saw them approach. Most of the other sellers only had what Sam or Barney told them was in the day's headlined.

Sam picked up a bell and held it high. "Not today he doesn't, Staples. Barney isn't selling any papers today.

As he brought bell down, signaling the end of the distribution time, 6AM, Barney skidded to a stop in front of the platform. He put his arm on it as he tried to catch his breath.

"Tol' ya, Barney'd make it!" Staples said. "Tol' ya myself even." He narrowed his eyes at Sam. "And as a goop, I can tell you you're a big goop yerself."

"I'm warning you, Staples," Sam scowled down at the boy.

"Right Barney?"

"The name's Honus." Barney said.

"Sure, sure thing. Honus." Staples grinned. "Doesn't roll off the tongue as well as Barney, but sure. How about I call you B-H? Ya got a middle name to round out your initials? Ya know, now that I think on it, a D would be handy if you add that. How about Dennis? Wha'da ya say B-D-H?"

Honus stared at Staples.

"Catchin' your breath?" Staples tried. He smiled. "Thinkin' if y'should have it put on yer luggage?"

"Don't got luggage."

"Well, if y'get any," Staples winked, "put it on there. In a nice fancy script. Gold letters even. Makes you look bonified."

Sam kicked Honus' arm off the platform. "Taking your time, *Barney*?"

"The name's Honus. We selling papers or not?"

"You're selling alright." Sam said. "Thanks to Staples; if it were up to me, you'd be panhandling today." Secretly he was relieved- Barney sold as many papers as any two other sellers and his father would not have been pleased to have that many papers not sell from his account.

"Right?" Staples hooked his thumbs on his suspenders. "I got to take care of my lackeys."

"What?" Honus glanced at Staples. "Who says I'm your lackey?"

"I do."

"So how many papers you want today, Mister Late Great Barney?" Sam interrupted. "You two can argue about who's in charge of your lame brains later."

"I'm in charge," Staples said. He jerked a thumb at his friend. "My lame brain's twice as good as Honus', here."

"Two bundles." Honus said flatly. He held up two fingers. "Two is this many, you lame brain."

"Yeah, that's right; you're the lame brain." Staples said with a grin. "Everyone knows it too."

"There's no credit, *Barney*," Sam said in a business tone. Even though he was their best seller, Sam still refused to call him

3

anything but his given name. And he had gone through several names in the two years he had been in town. "It's cold hard cash to sell, you know that."

A murmur went up from the other sellers- it was an unusually large amount of papers and an equally large outlay of cash.

"Yeah." Honus said. "I know that."

"That'll be four dollars. Even."

Honus nodded at Sam. "I've got it right here." Honus said casually as he pulled four quarters from his vest pocket. He pinched them between two fingers and held them high for Sam to take as he reached into his pocket with his other hand and pulled out three wrinkled dollar bills. "Easy money." He smiled even though he had scrimped and saved a month to come up with it.

Sam's eyes swiveled to the bell still in his hand. He slammed it down on the crate next to him. "Fine. Come get your papers." He waved at the others. "Toe the line!"

As they did every morning, they lined up to buy as many papers as they could afford to. They bought them for two cents then sold them for five. It would garner a tidy profit if it weren't for the fact that the Independent (and all other papers) would not buy back any unsold copies. A bad day selling would mean a large stack of worthless papers and little to eat. And worse- less papers to buy the next day causing a downward spiral that was all too familiar to many of them.

"Why ya need so many pape's?" Staples asked as he worked his way into line behind Honus. "Why, huh?"

"I got my reasons."

"You got some sort of plan, Barney?" Staples elbowed the other in the back.

4

"Honus. My name's Honus." Honus insisted.

"Sorry; Honus."

"I know I just said it. Just now."

"I weren't payin' attention; thought it was for the narrative." Admitted Staples.

"Well, it's Honus. Everyone else is keeping up, you should join them."

"Sure, sure, Honus. Got a plan, Honus?" He waggled his eyebrows. "Wanna let ol' Staples in on it"

"Not really."

Staples pursed his lips. "He had a good game, huh?" Staples elbowed his friend again. "Two hits and a stolen base even."

Honus nodded. "Yeah. Tried to get into the viewing party at the Blind Tiger."

"Da Blind Tigah!" Staples exclaimed. "Who you know to get in dere?"

"I couldn't get in." Honus said sourly. "Again."

"Yeah? Y' contacts couldn't get ya in?" He poked his friend again. "That it?"

Honus shoved him. "Quiet you! I don't know anyone. That's why I couldn't get in."

"Sure, sure, Honus. Whatever y'say." Staples leaned in close and whispered into Honus' ear. "So what's wit all the pape's?"

"I'm leaving."

"Ohhhh." Staples winked. "Headin' west? Go see what there is to see?"

"I'm going East."

"Most folks go West." Staples said. "Go West young man. Find adventure. Ya know? No more explorin' 'n adventurin' East. Pretty much all filled up over there on the right side of the map."

"Well, there's not any baseball out West." Honus said as the line moved forward. "Probably never will be. Too sophisticated for them."

"Right, right; too sophisticated for them cow wranglers to get the nuances." He elbowed Honus again. "So, baseball, huh? No more following in the footsteps of Sir Henry Morton Stanley? Trudgin' through South Africa even?" For the better part of four months, Barney had worn a pith hat he had found in a trash bin and demanded he be called Stanley.

Honus gave his friend a hard stare. "Things change."

"Baseball." Staples shook his head. "Y'know, I've never been to a game. Can ya make a livin' at that? A good livin'?"

"Better than selling pape's." He turned to look at his friend. "I'm going to bust if I don't get out of here."

"Bust, huh? Ya got a plan? What's the plan 'cause I know you got one."

"I'm goin' to Pittsburg."

"Well, there's something you don't hear every day." Staples put one hand over his heart. The other he held out above his head. "I'm going to seek my fortune in foreign lands. Exotic lands. In Pittsburg!"

Honus poked Staples in the chest. "And I'm not going to miss you at all."

Staples kept his pose. "And when I gets to Pittsburg, the first thing I'm going to do is miss good old Staples. He's the brains of the operation, you know."

"We don't have an operation."

"Oh yes," Staples continued, "head of the whole operation and I miss him dearly."

"No, I'm not... won't."

Staples put his hands on his hips. "So, it's settled; ya goin' to miss me." He rocked back on his heels. "Understandable."

"When you two are done talkin' 'bout nuthin'," snapped the Sam, "You can get t'work." He hefted a bundle of papers.

"I believe I'm going to miss you least of all," remarked Honus.

The boy tossed the bundle of papers at Staples.

Staples staggered back as he caught the bundle. "Thanks Sam, for being so considerate in throwing them to me. You are a tribute to your kind."

"Kind of what?" Honus said with a smirk, feeding his friend a straight line, nice and slow. Right over the plate.

Staples swung for the fences: "The proud and noble goop ruffian." He took a small bow.

"Pick yers up so you don't make a mess." Sam gestured at the large bundles.

Honus obliged by grabbing a bundle in each hand. He grunted as he pulled them off the platform. He swung them to get turned around then stumbled to the far wall of the alley. He dropped the bundles there and flexed his fingers.

Staples followed close behind his friend. He dropped his bundle as well. "So what we gots today, Honus? What we got?"

"Give me a minute, will ya?" Honus pulled the top paper out from one of the bundles carefully so he didn't tear the thin paper.

"Whatever you say, Honus." Staples sat on his stack. "Take your time."

Several other youths came to join them, also sitting on their papers. They didn't worry about ruining the bottom one or two; they never sold them all anyway.

"Let's see," Honus said as he scanned the front page. "Commodore Dewey defeated the Spaniards in Manila Bay."

"What? You're making that up!" Staples leaned forward. "It's over that quick? Hard t' believe."

"Whose side are you on?" One of the other boys shoved Staples- who happened to be fairly olive-skinned and distinctly darker than the other youths. "You a Castilian or something?" He tilted his head back and crowed. "Staples the Castilian cock!" He flapped his arms to add to the effect. And insult.

Staples frowned. Truth be told, he didn't know who his parents were or where they were from. He was definitely aware of his olive skin but didn't speak with any discernable accent besides 'street rat'. "I'm American, James." He shoved the other back. "I just didn't think it would be over so quick."

James blinked at Staples. "What? Who says the war's over?"

Staples pointed at Honus, who was now reading the article, "He said the Spaniards were *defeated*. That means it's over."

"The war's over, Barney?" James asked.

Honus looked up. "What are you two on about? Who said the war was over?"

"You did!" James and Staples said in unison.

"I just said that we beat them in Manila; that's just one battle. The article says we won there and there are plans to invade Cuba next. The war's not over."

"Oh." Staples elbowed James. "But we're going to win though."

"We? Who's we?" James leaned in on Staples.

"The Americans!" Staples shot back. "That's who! That's what we do. We won the Revolutionary War and the Civil War, didn't we?"

"Not the one in 1812," James countered. "We lost that one."

"If you two are done discussing American history," Honus said, "we can get to selling pape's."

"Yeah, Honus here needs to get going to fortune and glory." Staples winked. "In Pittsburg."

James started to speak, then just shook his head instead.

"Battle won in Manila," Honus said. "Spanish navy routed."

The youths repeated what Honus said to commit it to memory.

"Plans to invade Cuba in the works. Willie Simms wins the Kentucky Derby riding Plaudit." Honus looked at the youths. "Want another?"

"Got an easy one?" One boy said.

"Heavy storms called for later this afternoon and continue through the week. Tornado destroys houses in Ashland."

"Where's that?" Asked a girl.

"About forty miles east of here. The storms are moving west, towards us from over there." Honus pointed east.

"Who's calling for storms?" Staples asked with a smile. "Not very cordial, if you ask me."

Honus exhaled loudly. "I'm going to sell my papers." He stood and picked up both bundles. "See you goons this afternoon."

"Before the storms." Staples winked. "Right?"

James stood as well. "Well, if the storms do show up, we can count on Staples to crow and let us know." He slapped his knee then crowed. "Like that."

Staples stood quickly. He was a full head shorter than James.

"Got somethin' else to say?" James said, looking down at him.

Staples picked up his bundle of papers and stared at James for a moment. Then nodded to Honus, gave him a: "Sir." And walked off.

James crowed again.

Honus shoved James with his shoulder. "Lay off him, James." He turned to face James.

Honus was a good four inches taller than James and was a bit more muscular.

James smiled widely at him. "Don't get soaked today, Honus." He picked up his stack of papers. "Spaniards routed in Manila!" He shouted as he moved off. "Storms later today! Tornadoes destroy houses in Ashland! Panic ensues!"

With that, the youths moved off to their preferred paper-hawking areas and did their best to sell every one.

No one ever sold every single paper, though.

Only one got close- Honus.

~~~~~~~~~~~~~~~~~~~~~~~~~~~~~

"Never thought to trade like that," Staples said. "Definitely something I'll remember for later because es Bueno." He

10

smiled. "That means it's good in Spanish. I had a fellow tell me that when I told them about them Spaniards getting walloped."

Honus just nodded- he was exhausted from the day's work. He had managed to sell all but eleven of the papers. And those he had traded at the fish market for two smoked trout. "The pet shop'll take them too but all you can get out of him is petting the puppies and kittens."

Staples nodded. "I'm gonna remember that. Pet the kittens. Not the puppies though. Don't care much for dogs. They'll chase you without any good reason, ya know?"

Honus just nodded again. He was tired and wanted just to go to bed even though he knew there was no way that would happen. Mainly because he wasn't in control of his life. Yet.

The pair walked down the busy street eating and chatting as they went.

Dark storm clouds moved toward them from the East.

After ten minutes. Honus and Staples stopped in front of a large, dilapidated house. It was striking because the house had been built along with all the others on the street but it still looked a hundred years older.

Staples pushed the last of his smoked trout into his mouth. "Dinnerfm?" He chewed quickly.

"You're going to choke doing that one day. A stray bone's going to kill you."

"Can't let Miss Devinell see me eatin' meat."

"No, I suppose not," Honus said. "That's why I ate more and talked less while we walked here." He elbowed his friend.

"You saying I talk a lot?"

"What, now? Presently?"

"Yeah."

Honus smiled. "Well, besides not getting a word in edge-wise, I'd say... yes."

Now Staples elbowed Honus. "You think it's dinner time yet?"

Honus shrugged. "Not unless someone else did our chores for us. Can't imagine Miss Devinell's going to give us a free ride on them today."

As if on cue, a very tall blonde woman stormed through the front door. It clattered on worn hinges as it banged against the house- adding another couple of small dents to the overall battered look of it. Without shoes, she was an impressive six feet tall. Thanks to always wearing full Wellingtons- handmade of course, she gained an additional two inches above that- allowing her to tower over all but a handful of the male townsfolk and definitely all the females.

"Oh boy; she's wearing the purple Bespokes." Staples said out of the side of his mouth. "Here we go."

"Ya'll better get in 'here and git to yore chores!" She bellowed. Even her voice was bigger than everyone else's. "Dinner's in twenty minutes so you'uns better get a move on!"

"Yes, Miss Devinell," the two boys said in unison. They knew better than to talk back. Not only would Miss Devinell make sure they missed their dinner- which she was an expert at having them miss- she would also fetch the switch she often carried like a riding crop while out and about. She never missed with it either.

"Let's go, Honus." Staples said. "Work begun is half done is what they say."

"There's only proper names in *my* home! Proper is what we do here!"

"Ahh, then let us go Master Barney," Staples said with a smile. "Our duties doth await." He gave a short bow and gestured towards the uneven stairs. "In yon abode, no less."

"It's more than an abode," said Honus. He put his hand on his heart and recited:

> *Once more unto the breach, dear friend, once more-*
> *Or close the home up with our orphaned dead.*
>
> *In peace, there's nothing so becomes a boy and his chores.*
> *As modest stillness and humility shines like the floors.*

Staples looked at his friend- agog.
Miss Devinell narrowed her eyes.

> *But when the blast of Miss Devinell blows in our ears*

Honus continued.

> *Then imitate the action of the servant;*
>
> *stiffen the brushes,*
> *summon up the soap,*
>
> *and dispose the vile dust with hard-favored rags.*

"When you have had quite enough, *Henry.*" Miss Devinell said icily.

13

"What?" Staples said. "Who's Henry? You Henry, Honus… err, Barney?"

"It's Shakespeare," Honus said. "Sort of. It's mostly from a play called Henry the Fifth."

"Fifth of what?"

"He's the fifth Henry."

"I'm gonna be the brass cannon on you both if you don't get a move on!" Bellowed Miss Devinell. A rare smile played across her face. "So, get thee both to a broom closet."

Honus stifled a chuckle. "Yes, Miss Devinell."

"What?"

"Let's go." Honus grabbed Staples and pulled him into the house, past their towering matron.

~~~~~~~~~~~~~~~~~~~~~~~~~

At dinner, Honus sat opposite Staples at the front of the table since they were the oldest. The other dozen or so children formed a ring around the rest of the table with the youngest as far away from Miss Devinell as she could put them.

Rumbles of thunder made the younger children look at the ceiling.

An elderly black woman backed into the dining room through the large swinging door. She was pulling a cart.

"Evenin' all" she said as swung around to push the cart to the table.

In unison, the children -young and old- responded: "Good evening Miss Permilla."

14

"And how is every'un doin' this fine evening?"

"As fine as fine can be 'xpected under the circumstances," Staples said with a wide grin. "Circumstances being what they are."

"Them circumstances gotta be what they is; can't be nuthin else," Miss Permilla said as she wheeled the serving cart beside Miss Devinell. "What say you?" She asked her. "Ma'am?"

Miss Devinell sat at the head of the table in a tall, ornate chair that was on the verge of becoming a throne. She gave a sidelong glance to the black woman. "I'm sure I told you not to encourage the children."

Miss Permilla waved a hand dismissively as she picked up a large ladle. "Well, that's the main thing what children need, Ma'am; a good bit of encouragement."

"All's I can say is you encourage me t' eat with your fine cooking," Staples said, even though the cooking was all in all bland and completely free of meat.

No one was sure why Miss Devinell did not eat meat but the theories abounded- from having worked in a slaughter house as a child to being deathly allergic to meat and anything in between. However, above all, one thing was certain- none of the children had the courage to ask her why it was never served.

"Well that's mighty kind of you, Staples." Miss Permilla rounded the end of the table and headed back up the other side.

One of the shutters on the dining room windows clattered against the frame.

"Oh!" Staples said. "There's storms heading this way." He nodded at Barney. "The paper said so. All of them did, in fact."

"Really?" Miss Devinell asked. "Big storms?"

"They got's t'a be," said Permilla. "My bunion's been swearin' at me all day long." She ladled vegetable stew into bowls as she pushed the cart around the table. "Givin' me a hard time is what they is been doin'."

"Well, if you can't trust Miss Permilla's bunions, we got bigger troubles," Staples smiled wide. "Am I right, or am I right?"

The smallest of the children at the end of the table giggled.

Miss Permilla hushed them as she rolled by, ladling vegetable stew as she went.

The shutter banged against the window again as the wind picked up.

"The paper talked about tornadoes." Barney said. "Wiped out several houses in Ashland."

"That's not all that far," remarked Miss Devinell. "Oh dear."

"Not how the crow flies, anyhow," Staples said. "Unless they gots a headwind."

Miss Devinell looked at the window as the shutter banged again. "If nothing else, that shutter needs to be fastened before it breaks that window." She looked at Barney. "If you would please."

Barney looked down at his hot stew. "Can I eat first then…" he was interrupted by the shutter banging again.

"Not unless you earned enough to replace that window because of your dawdling."

Staples guffawed. "I'll let'cha know how the hot stew was!"

"Mister Jay, why don't you assist your associate?"

16

"Why?" Staples looked down at his stew. "Because when all is said 'n done, I'd rather eat my stew."

"Mister Jay," Miss Devinell repeated. "As the two eldest here, I would like to think you would both be glad to help."

"I'd be glad to help myself to some hot stew."

The children at the end of the table giggled again.

"Come on, Staples," Honus said. "If we're quick about it we can get them all before it gets too cold." He stood and pulled his friend up with him.

The wind whistled outside as it suddenly became darker in the room.

"You boys better hurry on and git back indoors!" Permilla said as she rubbed her hands together. "That wind's startin' to do some real yelling out there."

Without further coaxing, the two boys left the dining room.

"Eat up kids, then we're all gittin' in the cellar." Miss Permilla said.

"That is a fine idea," Miss Devinell said.

"Will you tell us ghost stories again?" One of the smaller children asked. "Pleeease?"

"If you all et your food up quick so I can git the kitchen tidy, I shore will." Miss Permilla said.

The shutter slammed hard against the window frame as the wind took up a menacing moan.

"Perhaps the kitchen can wait until later," Miss Devinell said as she stood. "We will all take our soup to the cellar and eat there. Follow me please."

"I'll follow along behind, Ma'am," Permilla said. She looked out the window- it was very dark out. "Land sakes it's gone dark out there! Those boys better hurry on up!" She moved around the table and picked up the two boys' bowls. "Git moving kids!"

Single file, the children followed the headmistress to the basement, Permilla bringing up the rear.

~~~~~~~~~~~~~~~~~~~~~~~~~~~

Honus pushed out the front door as the wind fought to keep it closed. "You go left and I'll go right," Honus said over the wind. "Meet you at the chicken coop. We'll close it up then head inside." He looked up at the sky. It was dark with clouds that seemed to be boiling.

"Meet ya with the other chickens!" Staples said as he slapped Honus' shoulder. "Tag, yer it!" He ran to the first window beside the front door and fought to get the shutters closed.

Honus went the opposite direction, latching shutters as he went.

After several minutes of struggling with windows, Honus rounded the corner to the back of the house- a dozen closed windows behind him. Ahead, thanks to a long hallway along the back of the house, there were only three windows left. He leaned forward against the wind and struggled to the first window. The windward side slapped shut so quickly it caught his hand. Honus winced as he pulled his hand from between the shutter and the frame. He leaned back and forced the other shutter to cover the glass. When it was there, he flipped the hasp over its eyelet, giving it a twist to make sure it stayed put.

As he fought to reach the other window, Staples came around the far corner. The wind pushed him almost past the first

18

window in front of him. As he fought with that window, Honus got the middle one secured. He stayed in place as Staples half slid, half ran to him.

"There's a train coming, Honus!" Staples yelled into his friend's ear. "Those people are in trouble if they get off!"

"There's no tracks around us!" Honus yelled back over the wind. He looked up at the pitch-black sky. "Tornado!" He shouted. "It's a tornado!" He pointed at the chicken coop. "Let's get in there!" He leaned forward against the wind. "Before we get blown down the block!"

Staples shook his head. "Cellar!" He pointed in the direction Honus had come- there was an outside entrance to the cellar. "Get to the cellar!"

"We'll never get those doors open!" Honus shouted back. "The coop!" He took a step towards the chicken coop. Something past it caught his eye. It was a piece of heavy wooden fence floating in the air. It seemed to hover in place then disappeared up into the blackness. Honus' eyes got large when he realized that the fence disappeared into the roiling mass of a monstrous tornado. "Staples!" He shouted. When he looked back, he saw his friend struggling to open the cellar door against the wind. He would get it a couple of inches up, then the wind would slam it down again. He seemed to know better than to try opening the other door- lest he never get it shut again.

The sound was deafening as the tornado approached. Honus leaned forward and rushed to the only cover near him- the chicken coop. He pushed himself through the narrow door then poked his head out and looked for his friend. Staples was now leaning forward against the wind, trying to get to the chicken coop. "Hurry, Staples!"

The wind tilted the coop onto its side, toward Staples. As it did, Honus fell to the far wall. It tumbled again as chickens flew around squawking. "Staples!" He shouted over the din as the coop flipped onto its roof.

As Honus fell forward, he put his hands out to catch himself. Relieved he wasn't hurt, he flopped over onto his butt, directly over the now-blocked door.

He looked up just as the heavy boards the chickens sat on, fell forward on him.

Chapter 2 - Not Kansas

The witch looked out at the colorful valley from the broad balcony that circled her majestic ivory-white tower. It was tall enough that several clouds passed below where she was standing.

"And I'm not even on the top floor," she observed with a satisfied tone.

Everything seemed peaceful- just like she liked it. Order and discipline. And quiet.

Especially quiet.

A peal of thunder rumbled past.

Especially quiet, damned it all!

She stalked to a far corner of the balcony and looked into the distance. Far off to the West, the clear blue skies turned dark. Black clouds circled over a similarly dark castle. Flashes of lightning caused the clouds to glow grey and purple as they danced across them. Occasionally a bolt would run jagged to the ground. Where she was sure it disturbed a weed-infested ground without any flowers planted in nice neat rows.

She squinted at the castle.

"You have *got* to be kidding me." She said to no one in particular. Particularly because no one was around. She added a long sigh just because she felt it helped establish the mood better. "What are you up to now? That stupid broom just isn't going to hold any more magic."

With a flourish of her ample blue skirt, she turned and stalked through the ornate crystal double doors to her bedroom. Her bright blue and lace bedroom. As she passed through, she straightened a vibrant blue pillow on a light blue sofa. She pushed through a pair of swinging crystalline doors into her Scrying Chamber.

Hugging the wall to avoid the large map and realistic, yet tiny model buildings that took up almost the entire area, she made her way to a small staircase that led to a platform. Besides a bright green caldron (it was this year's black when it came to caldrons), the platform was empty, giving her a clear view of the entire map below.

As they always did, bubbles rose from various parts of the map.

Blue bubbles signified balance in the Ether.

Balance in the Ether was as important as peace and quiet.

Damned important!

Occasional pink bubbles would rise and noiselessly pop- those were minor arguments. The darker they were, the more heated the issue was. She looked at the far corner. Purple bubbles rose steadily from a two-foot tall, exact duplicate castle of the one

22

she had just squinted her eyes at. She squinted her eyes at this one too. Just in case the previous squinting had worn off.

"Honestly; just a week of peace and quiet. Is that too much to ask?" She picked up her long wooden wand and reached out for a purple bubble. As it settled on the end of the wand, she gently pulled it close and peered into it. Inside she could see a female figure dressed in all black robes (black was last year's black that also worked this year, when it came to robes Especially before Labor Day.). She was bent over a caldron. A black caldron. She was stirring it with a broom handle.

"That broom just will not hold any more magic." The Blue Witch said again. "*You moron*," she added.

She was well aware that of the three adversarial witches that lived nearby, this one was the most persistent.

Which was a problem.

She wasn't by any means the most powerful, but the Blue Witch was well aware that persistence could make up for lack of talent more often than not. If the witch who lived in the west was able to figure out how to hold more magic in her broom, she would definitely prove to be a threat. And, the Blue Witch thought sourly, she would no longer be able to taunt her with a trite 'Be gone, you have no power here' because she *would* have power. Everywhere. Everywhere her broom would fly her. Which included very tall, above-the-clouds ivory towers.

That was a problem.

Also a problem was the witch in the East who was fairly lazy when it came to magic. With exercise, she was maniacal and determined. Unfortunately, she was also quite talented- at magic. And, as the Blue Witch knew all too well, sometimes talent could make up for a lackadaisical attitude because problems would be solved quickly or even on the first try. That

witch was also trying to extend her powers to include the realm of the Blue Witch.

The Blue Witch laughed. "With shoes, no less."

It was true that the Witch of the East did indeed have a broom and was able to fly on it over most every part of the lands, but that was the extent of its power. Deciding that trying to pack more magic into a broom was a fool's mission, she decided to use highly conductive silver incorporated into a pair of slippers. They would be easy to carry, simple to use, and more importantly, go with almost everything. Unfortunately, the Witch of the East learned that while silver was an excellent conductor; it did not store Magical Ether for very long- only a matter of hours, in fact.

She grappled with the tradeoff because of aesthetic reasons. But in the end, she had to find another storage option- fashion be damned.

Highly-efficient Magic Ether storing rubies replaced the silver on the shoes. With great success. The tradeoff in this case was that the Witch of the East now needed to make sure she wore something else red: a sash, a ribbon on her pointed hat, or lipstick even, to make sure the outfit pulled together well.

All powerful magic was a great thing. Being able to use it while looking good was even greater.

The greatest, in fact.

Which brought up the very real and all too close danger. The Witch of the South.

The Blue Witch panned her gaze around the map. True enough, there were darker bubbles coming from South as well. Not as dark as the other directions, but that was unfortunately because the Witch of the South had already perfected her Magic Ether Talisman- a crystalline star pendant. If the other two of the Cardinal Witch Coven ever got their projects working properly, the Blue Witch knew her days were numbered.

In single digits.

As a self-identified Good Witch (good was this year's black), this caused problems as the outright killing of another Witch (Especially of the same Coven) was frowned upon and would definitely be addressed at the annual Witches and Warlocks Extravaganza (where you only needed the edge of the bench it was so exciting).

Throttling all three of the witches with her bare hands was very near the top of her 'Things I'd love to do to those stinking Cardinal Witch Coven witches if I could get away with it and not have to pay a fine and listen to a lecture at the WWE event' list.

Of course, the only reason it wasn't at the top was because by the time she wrote 'Things I'd love to do to those stinking Cardinal Witch Coven witches if I could get away with it and not have to pay a fine and listen to a lecture at the WWE event' on the parchment, 'Choke the life out of each and every one of them with my bare hands while I stare into their eyes until they go stone cold' was two lines down.

Underneath that was "Run them over with a wagon from sunrise to sunset, then an extra hour just in case it's not the solstice." The methods became decidedly more gruesome after those rather mild killing methods.

The Blue Witch squinted at the map. She raised her hands up, fingers splayed out. "Hate, hate, and hate," she said, using her Oxfordian Comma Incantation for extra emphasis. "If only I could…"

A black bubble materialized above the map.

Unlike the other bubbles that all percolated upward, this one appeared almost twenty feet above it (Vaulted ceilings were this year's haute ceilings). And hovered.

"What?"

The Blue Witch reached out with her wand then hesitated. The last -and only- time a black bubble appeared over her map was when *He* arrived a decade ago. She moved around the map trying to determine where it would land as the black bubble bobbed around. Unlike last time, it was not heading for the Emerald City.

"Thank goodness!" She put her hand on a grassy knoll next to the Ozonian Book Repository and leaned out to look closely at the bubble, careful not to touch it. There was a young man spinning in it. Spinning inside a large wooden box. As she leaned back, the bubble started to slowly descend. "Where to now?" She leaned back to get a better perspective on its trajectory. "Nexus Village? Those little *dolts*." True to her prediction, the bubble, which was now elongated and spinning, was heading to where the Red and Yellow Brick Roads started. Or ended. Or perhaps they spiraled out in different directions from there after coming out of the ground. Either way, it was known as The Nexus.

As she watched, the bubble spun faster, hollowing out to become a funnel. "No, no, no! Not now! Not yet!" She turned and ran to the balcony. When she got there, she waved her wand in front of her in a broad circle. As it moved, a shimmering in the air took form, enveloping her in a translucent bubble of Magic Ether. Silently it lifted off the balcony and with no regard for the wind at all, moved northward to The Nexus.

The Blue Witch stole a glance toward the distant black castle in the West (mountains kept her from seeing the matching one in the East) to see if anything had changed. The clouds still flashed with lightning. "Keep busy with your broomifying endeavors." Then a thought occurred to her. She looked East, then West, then South. "What if…" she said aloud, "what if this one is like the last? Then it's three against three!"

It was no secret that the Wizard that had arrived a decade ago in a similarly absurd fashion had no love for any of the witches- the Blue Witch included. But, of the four of them, she was the most reasonable- and supposedly less treacherous. It was the lace that made people incorrectly think that. (Lace was this year's white)

"If I can get this one to help with even one of them, then perhaps between *Him* and I, we can deal with the remaining two." She looked ahead to Nexus City then up at the sky. There was a dark patch where ostensibly the new visitor was already falling to the ground. "But which one to set you on?" While the old man was formidable in his own mysterious way, the Blue Witch was unsure of his actual power. And range. The East and West witches were closer which meant she could deal with them easier- the most powerful of the Cardinal Coven was without a doubt, the Witch of the South. She was also farthest away- several days' walk. Much too far for the Witch of the North to effectively deal with her in person.

The Blue Witch looked southward. "I shall have to see if I can coax this one to deal with *you*, dear sister." She looked forward again and concentrated on moving as quickly as possible. She would need all the time she could get to convince the bumbling citizens of Nexus Village to do anything even remotely helpful. And to keep them from singing.

Especially to keep them from singing.

Chapter 3 -Still not Kansas

The chicken coop landed with a hearty thud atop a topiary of the mayor of Nexus Village.

The small man sleeping beside it opened one eye. He peered at the crumpled and upside-down chicken coop leaning against the topiary. "A definite improvement on the likeness of our esteemed elected official through the addition of mixed media." He closed his eye. "Hell, that's practically art now."

~~~~~~~~~~~~~~~~~~~~~~~~~~

After a few minutes, Honus opened his eyes. Boards and straw were piled on him. He tried pushing himself up but the large roosting shelves that had fallen on him were too heavy. "Help?" He called.

The small man sleeping beside the crumpled topiary opened one eye. He looked around.

"Miss Devinell? I'm stuck!"

Not being a Miss, or named Devinell, or caring about someone being stuck, the small man closed his eye. Tightly.

Honus pushed himself forward into the open space ahead of him. As he did, boards behind him stayed propped up, giving him a place to leverage his legs. Alternating between pushing with his legs, and pulling with his arms, he was able to get to the outer wall of the chicken coop. Exhausted, he stopped to catch his breath.

The small man sleeping beside the crumpled topiary started to snore.

After another few moments, Honus tried to push himself into a standing position but there wasn't room. He looked up to appraise his situation when he realized that he was against the front door of the coop. It was half ajar but couldn't open farther because it was still latched.

"Anyone out there?" Honus called.

The little man opened his eye and swiveled it toward the mixed-medium art. Being a definite someone and not just anyone, he closed his eye again.

Honus stretched his arm up but the latch was just out of reach. He pulled his legs up under himself and pushed upward, gaining the precious inches he needed to reach the latch. He pulled down on it.

Nothing happened.

"Come on," Honus said. Then he realized the coop was upside down. He pushed up on the latch and the door sprung open, hanging loosely by the lower hinge. "Miss Devinell? Miss Permilla?"

"Those women ain't here, sonny," said the small, no longer sleeping man. His eyes were still shut though. "Course you're doing the talking equivalent of at least three womenfolk. Don't need no more tossed into the mix."

Honus looked out from the chicken coop. The area outside should have been flat and brown- it was anything but. "Where am I?" He crawled out of the chicken coop then stood. "Where did?" Words failed him. He was standing in a large circular intersection. A bright blue cobblestone road circled the chicken coop them ran off in four directions. The houses across the circle were squatty but colorful from their bright green grass to their canary yellow thatched roofs. A purple goat casually nibbled on the grass, not paying attention to him at all. "I don't think I'm in Kansas anymore." He remarked.

"Ya don't say?" The small man opened one eye. "What makes ya say that?"

"Kansas is mostly dingy. The parts that aren't, are drab. Now there are some parts downtown that are grimy and gaudy but nothing like this." He looked around. "Wow."

"This ain't Wow." The small man said as he opened an eye. He looked Honus up and down. "Not by a long shot." He pointed off to his right. "That's at the big bend in the Chocolate River, past the candy factory."

"What is this then?"

"Evidently it's the absolute *worst* spot to take a nap," the man snapped as he hopped to his little feet. Even the man's clothes were colorful. He picked up an equally-colorful top hat and put it on, tapping the top of it to push it down on his head. Which was covered with curly hair. Bright blue curly hair.

"Huh," Honus said as he watched the rotund midget dust himself off. "Curiouser and curiouser," he remarked.

"Hold it right there," the midget pointed a stubby finger at Honus. "Right. There."

"Where? Here?"

"I'd appreciate it if you didn't use that turn of a phrase around here."

Honus thought for a moment. "I'm not sure where here is, Sir."

The midget was taken aback. "Sir, you say? Sir? Well, I never."

Honus held his hands up, "I'm sorry, I meant no offense." He looked around. "Would you please tell me which way I ought to go from here?"

"Well, that depends a good deal on where you want to get to," the midget answered without thinking too much about it.

"I don't much care where…"

"Now stop it right there!" The midget pointed the stubby finger at Honus once again. "Didn't I tell you not to turn those phrases around here? Mixing things up like that." He tut-tutted. "Makes bad things happen. Got enough troubles around here with witches and wizards scheming to kill each other, and other odd folk with parts falling off without *you* muddying the puddle with some sort of drug-addled dream!"

Honus stared at the little man for a moment. "I don't even know how to answer that." He looked around. "Where, exactly am I…" he hesitated and offered: "Mister?"

The midget narrowed his eyes at the youth. "Well, I'll accept that." He dusted his hands together. "So, I'll answer your question." He pointed at the bright green grass at his feet. "You're right here, of course. At the absolutely worst spot to take a nap!" With that, he stomped off. "The nerve of some people!" He tossed over his tiny shoulder.

"Oh boy," Honus said as he looked around. "Where am I?"

"Hey!" A voice said.

"What?" Honus looked at the goat. "Did you say something?"

"Don't get *me* involved in this," the Goat said. "I'm just background ambiance, working for scale no less. Only got one line and that was it."

"Hey!" The voice said again.

32

Honus looked around. "Who's there?"

"Me!"

"Me who?"

There was a long pause then: "Well, me is who."

Honus looked at the chicken coop. "You're inside the coop?" He bent down and looked in the doorway.

"Get me outta here!" A voice said.

Honus got on his hands and knees. "I didn't think anyone followed me outside. Who's in there?"

"Me! We've established that already." The voice said. "Are you stupid or something?"

Honus crawled into the crushed structure up to his waist. "Where are you?"

"I seem to be upside down."

"All I see are some chicken legs sticking out of the hay."

The legs waggled back and forth.

"Are they moving?" Asked the voice.

"Huh; I suppose there are," Honus admitted. "How'd you know that?"

"Just a hunch."

Honus watched the chicken feet flail around. "Huh."

"Pull them out, huh."

Honus grabbed the flailing legs and pulled out a large, colorful rooster.

"Thought they were chicken feet."

33

"Want to know the easiest way to tell what kinda feet you're holding?"

"Sure?" Honus turned his head over to try and look at the Rooster's face right side up.

"Check to see what they're attached to."

"Huh."

"Thanks for that," said the Rooster. "Real sociable of you to be providing quality dialogue like that."

Honus stared at the rooster.

"If you find the time in the very near future to put me on the ground instead of holding me upsidedown..."

Honus let go.

The rooster bounced off his head and flopped to a side. "You realize I'm not a cat, right?" The Rooster said as he fluttered his wings and moved to his feet.

"Huh."

"Listen, kid," the Rooster said. "I appreciate your help and all but if we're going to go back around to 'huh' every time that..."

"You can talk!"

The rooster cocked his head to the side. "... every time that a stray thought gets into your head, we're never going to get anywhere."

"Where are we going?"

"Out of this upside-down coop for starters." The rooster took a little hop to land on Honus' back then strutted out.

Honus squirmed out of the chicken coop then sat down. "Hey, rooster, how can you talk?"

The rooster turned his head to the side and eyed Honus. "Why can you?"

"Because people talk, of course."

"You saying I'm not people?"

"You're a rooster."

"Roosters are people too," the rooster said. He looked around. "Where you heading, kid?"

Honus looked around as well. "I'm not too sure. Actually, I'm not too sure where I am, either."

"You're a mess. It's a good thing I'm in charge."

"You're in charge?" Honus said.

"That makes it unanimous." The Rooster pointed with its wing down one of the side streets. "We'll head that way."

"Why that way?" Honus pointed down another of the blue roads. "Why not that way."

"When you're in charge, you can make those kinds of decisions." The rooster started walking in the direction he had pointed. "Let's go."

"But..." Honus watched the rooster strut away. With a shrug, he got to his feet and jogged to catch up with the animal.

"Now you've got the idea." The rooster said.

"You got a name, rooster?"

"Rooster." Rooster continued to strut down the road.

Honus frowned. "Okay, I suppose."

"Well you don't get to suppose, kid. You don't get to pick other folks' names; just your own."

"I'm Bar... Honus."

"I didn't ask." Rooster said.

"Well, I just figured..."

"Fine, fine BarHonus. Wait; your name is BarHonus and you're giving *me* a hard time about 'Rooster'?"

"Sorry about that."

"Fine, BarHonus, don't go getting all mushy on me."

"It's just Honus." Honus said. "You sure are testy, Rooster."

"With a show of hands, who has been dropped on their head lately?"

The two walked in silence for a moment.

"I crash landed in a chicken coop," Honus finally said.

Rooster cocked his head at Honus. He opened his mouth, then closed it. He looked forward and continued to walk, muttering under his breath.

The blue road went up a small hill, as got close to the top, Honus could see a town beyond it. "Hey; there's a town up ahead."

"Nice. That's progress, then." Rooster said. He strutted faster. "Progress is what we got going on right here, Honus sidekick of mine."

"I don't see how I'm your sidekick. After all, I'm human."

"You saying Roosters aren't people?"

"Well, I mean... you're part of the chicken family, right? I don't see how you're in charge of anything just being a chicken and all."

"Welcome to Nexus City!" A rotund little man said as he hopped in front of the pair, stopping them. "Welcome! I'd just like to say that..."

"Be right with you." Rooster said to the little man. He turned to face Honus. "We're going to have it out at one point, you and me. I just want you to know that so you're not surprised when it happens."

"Well I..." Honus said. He looked between the little man and the roster. "Hello... Mister?"

"What's with the hesitation and the questioning tone?" The little man said as he put his hands on his very wide hips. "You think I look like a woman or something?"

"No, it's just that..." Honus began. "Lately..." He frowned.

"Don't feel bad, sir." The rooster brought his wing up to his mouth and continued in a loud whisper. "He doesn't know the difference between chickens and roosters either."

"Hey now..."

"Well, according to most experts," the little man said with a smile, "chickens lay eggs and roosters crow. Noble creature, the Rooster. Master of all they survey. Kings of their free range."

Rooster pointed a wing at the little man. "See? *That's* how you act around people. Remember that."

"I think that we got off on the wrong foot." Honus said.

"I'm Ned" said the rotund man. "The previously napping."

"Nice name you got there, Ned." Rooster said. "Pleasure to meet you, in fact." He looked up at Honus. "See? That's how polite folks talk. Give it a try."

"Hi." Said Honus.

Rooster shook his head. "Some people."

"Well, people are people no matter how... oh hell." The little man looked up at the sky above and behind Honus and Rooster.

"Well, that's a saying I haven't heard before; 'People are people no matter how oh hell.' You?" Rooster looked at Honus. "They say things like that where you come from?"

"Where I come from, Roosters don't talk and I've never talked to a midget. Seen one at the circus once."

The little man continued to look over the pair's head. "And it started as such a quiet day."

"You know, where I come from, not looking at folks when you talk to them is considered rude," Rooster said to the little man. "That's probably universal. Unless you're playing poker."

"Oh hell." Ned looked around. "Here we go again." He looked down at Rooster and Honus. "You two aren't wanted for... anything, are you?"

"Not me." Rooster said.

"What?" Honus asked. "Wanted for what?"

"Apparently my sidekick is unable to answer that question directly so I'm going to go out on a limb and say he's guilty of something."

"What? Me?" Honus looked back and forth between the little man and Rooster. "No, I didn't break the law.

"Now it sounds like someone's trying to justify something they did." Rooster looked at the little man. "What say you and I..."

Ned was running toward town.

"What is going on here?" Honus said.

38

Rooster craned his neck around and looked up at the sky. "Huh," He remarked.

"When I say things like that, you give me a hard time." Honus said tersely.

"Well, when *you* say it, there's nothing worthwhile going on to make that comment."

"Well what about...?" Honus started to look over his shoulder.

Rooster began to run after the little man.

A large blueish bubble was rapidly descending toward Honus in what looked like a broad arc if the trail of little bubbles behind it was any indication. Continuing the arc in front of it had it landing exactly where Honus was standing.

"What the?" Honus looked down to where Rooster had been standing. Startled he wasn't there, he looked around. When he saw that he was running after the little man, Honus started running too.

After just a few strides, he had caught up to Rooster. "Why are we running?"

"You ever heard that old saying 'eat where the locals eat'?"

"No, I can't say that I have. But I suppose it sounds like good advice."

"Well, it also pertains to when the locals run." Rooster said. "If you want to catch up with that little man, take me with you."

Honus bent down and grabbed Rooster by the neck and picked him up. Holding tight, he sprinted to catch up with the man. "Why are we running?" He said when caught up with him.

The little man -who was almost as wide as he was tall- was breathing hard as he ran as fast as he could. "She... she... coming." He managed to say. "Try...get... get... away."

"Urp," said Rooster.

Honus continued to run beside the man easily- it was really more of a jog for him thanks to the little man's sideways physique.

The trio finally reached the middle of town and the little man skidded to a stop. He pivoted to look the way they had come. "She's still coming," he said as he breathed hard. He tried to put his hands on his knees but his belly got in his way. He opted to just rest his elbows on his stomach instead. "Here we go again. I wonder what we did wrong this time."

Honus turned to look.

The blue bubble had adjusted its trajectory and was now still heading toward them, moving in a very fast, very unbubble-like manner.

"What is that?" Honus said.

"Urp," Rooster said.

"You'll go blind doing that," Ned remarked.

"What?" Honus did a double take at the little man.

The little man pointed at Rooster.

Honus looked at Rooster- he still had him by the neck.

Rooster's eyes were bulging out. "Urp!" He said again. His eyes seemed to be facing different directions.

Honus let go of Rooster.

Rooster flopped to the ground. "Oh, we're going to have it out!" He flapped his wings as he strutted back and forth, catching his breath. "We are *definitely* going to have it out!"

"This is absurd." Honus remarked. As the bubble reached them, he ducked.

Rooster stepped behind Honus' leg.

Ned continued to breathe deeply. From past experience he knew there wasn't really anything else he could do that would be helpful.

The bubble came to an abrupt halt just a foot above the ground. With a faint popping sound, it burst and a woman dressed in all blue fell the remaining distance to the ground. She performed a plie as she landed. "And *that's* how it's done. None of that flying around on an implement of cleaning or in a flash of fire that would probably burn you and put you out of commission for six weeks or so. Disgraceful. Uncouth even."

"Oh great and powerful Wit.... Mistress of the North," Ned said. He added as deep a bow as his belly would allow. "How great to have you bless our presence with..." He looked up. "Your presence?"

The Blue Witch narrowed her eyes at him, then looked at Honus. "Well, well, how nice of you to come, my scrumptiously tall young man." She said with a friendly, albeit disturbingly high-pitched and warbly voice. She coughed and cleared her throat then continued in a normal voice: "And your little friend too." She smiled at Rooster.

"Nice to meet you, Ma'am," Honus said, glad to finally have something close to a normal conversation.

The Blue Witch looked around. "Come out, come out wherever you are!" She said in a sing-song voice. "And meet our newest visitor." She waved her wand around, making Honus duck. "Who came from afar."

Much to Honus' surprise, several dozen similarly small people popped up from flower beds, from behind fences, and even from the little houses. "Huh." He said. Worried, he looked down at Rooster.

41

"No, you're right on the money this time." Rooster said. "Well done."

"Come welcome our visitor from afar." She pointed her wand at a particularly round man that had just stepped beside Honus. "Come Mayor, say hello and meet the young man who fell from a star."

Glad to be out of the scene, Ned slowly backed into a group of nameless extras.

"It was a chicken coop," Honus admitted.

"He fell from a coop, he fell very far," the Blue Witch said without missing a beat.

"In Kansas."

The Blue Witch's eyes lit up. "Oh? And *Kansas* he says is the name of the coop."

"Kansas is the name of your coop?" The Mayor said. He shrugged. "We don't name coops around here. He looked around. "What say you all?"

"Kansas, he says, is the name of his coop?" They all sang. They weren't buying it either.

"And do you bring good news from your coop in Kansas?" The Blue Witch asked, hoping for some sort of dark, witch-killing news.

"Well, there's not much good news in Kansas, normally. Kind of dull, really." Honus said. "In fact, I was in the process of leaving when the wind began to pick up, and my house was getting pitched around. And suddenly the shutters started to unhitch, so I went out to try and get them fastened shut so they didn't break a window."

The Blue Witch nodded approvingly. "Nice. If that sentence of anti-rhyming doesn't kill the song, nothing will. Mayor?"

The Mayor wrung his hands nervously as he approached. "Yes, yes, I suppose." He glanced over his shoulder. The other Munchkins were not smiling. The one thing his constituents liked the most was singing. Hoping to appease them he gave a short bow and tried to start another, approved-by-his-constituents song. "As Mayor of Nexus City, in the county and country of Oz, I'd like to welcome you to Munchkin Land."

"Tra-la-la-la. La-la-la," sang all the other little people happily. "Tra-la-la..."

The Blue Witch sighed. She hoped to get out of Nexus Village without a song. Or at least a complete song. "Yes, yes. Very nice, Mayor. Well done, even", she interrupted. She turned to face Honus. "So, what is it that you are here for?"

"I..." Honus looked down at Rooster. "Well, we are hoping to get back home to Kansas. Do you know how I can get there?"

The Blue Witch shuddered with joy. "Oh, I do indeed, my well-put-together young man. I do indeed."

"Tra-la-la-la. La-la-la", said the little people.

The blue witch raised a well-manicured eyebrow. "The best and easiest way to get back home is..."

"To ask the Wizard, of course," the Mayor said helpfully. He was on the brink of another town-wide song. "So just follow the Yellow..."

The Blue Witch shot the Mayor a look. It hit him right between the eyes and gave him an instant, pounding headache.

"But that's not really an option, now that I think about it." The Mayor added meekly as he rubbed his temples.

"Tra-la-la-la. La-la-la, la-la-la", said all the other little people.

Even Rooster joined in this time.

"Who's this Wizard?" Honus asked. "Can he help me?"

The Blue Witch shook her head. "Sadly, no. He's away on holiday. Gone for an indeterminate amount of time to an undisclosed location with no way to reach him. Your best bet is..." She looked East then West. Then South. "Is to go South. There is a very powerful witch there who has a magical talisman that can get you home."

"What's a talisman?" Honus asked. He smirked. "Magic? Really?"

The Blue Witch smiled sweetly at him. "Oh yes, it's very magical and powerful and will get you home. All you have to do is take it from her and..."

"Well, I don't steal," Honus said, "that's something I've never done."

"Tra-la-la-la. La-la-la", said Rooster. He looked around. "Oh, sorry. I thought I was getting the hang of the chorus." He moved beside Honus. "So we... *borrow*" he winked slowly, "this magical talisman thing from this Witch," he looked up and nodded at Honus, "with plans to return it as soon as we are done with it, and even include a thank you note. Then what?"

"Then you use it to get back home." The Blue Witch said. "Obviously."

"And she's going to just let us use this thing?" Honus said, unconvinced.

"Well, she's a very bad witch, that one. She torments the poor citizens all around." The Blue Witch wheeled on the Mayor and pointed at him with her wand. "Isn't that true, *Mister Mayor*?"

The Mayor hopped backward. "Oh yes, she's the worstest of them all, that one." He lied. "I can't imagine how things could get worse around here if she wasn't tempering the

44

current...Ahhh, with her tormenting us all the time." Actually, out of all the witches, the Witch of the South was the one that came around the least- she hadn't been in town for over a year. That was when she had happened by during their annual bar-b-cue and left in disgust when she saw them roasting a very large boar. "Why I remember the last time she..."

"See?" The Blue Witch said sweetly. "So just swipe her talisman and use it to get home. You and your little rooster."

"What's a talisman?" Honus said again.

The Blue Witch took a deep breath. Then a second with her eyes closed. For the third one, she opened her eyes since she had gained control of her fury. "Well," she said finally, "Not that I know exactly what it is but if I were to guess, I'd say it was a five pointed star looking crystal with gems set in it, that she wears around her neck on a long gold chain so it sits right between her breasts as if she really needed something to bring attention to them sitting there all natural and perky, like perfect porcelain D-cups." Her smile had turned into a frown as she spoke. It returned as she said: "I guess."

"So how do we get it?" Honus asked. "If she wears it around her neck."

"Figure something out," the Blue Witch said flatly. "Something really most sincerely terminal, if at all possible."

"Got it," Rooster said. "Find this witch. Take her star. Do a piece of work on her if we need to. Go home."

"How do we find her?" Honus said. "Is it far, her home?"

The Blue Witch grasped her wand tightly pretending she was choking the young man in front of her to death. When she got to the point where his bulging eyes became lifeless, she said: "It's very simple since you find yourself in Nexus Village, my tasty young man." She panned her long wooden wand over her

45

head and then brought the hilt of it down at her feet. The rapport it made reverberated off the tiny houses. "Start right here." She looked at the spiral at her feet- the red and yellow roads started right there in a tight spiral and went off in different directions. She knew that the yellow one led to the Wizard but that wouldn't solve her problem. Yet. The red one would lead directly to the Witch of the South. "You just follow the Red Brick Road." She said cheerily.

"Follow the Red Brick Road?" Honus said as he looked down at the spiral of the two roads.

"Follow the Red Brick Road!" The Mayor affirmed. It wasn't the most popular song but it was in the top ten. Especially during the holidays.

"Tra-la-la-la. La-la-la," said Rooster.

Several of the little people nodded. "Follow the red brick road," they all said in unison.

"And at the end of the road is where..." Honus began.

"FOLLOW THE RED BRICK ROAD!" Screeched the Blue Witch.

Honus ducked. "All right, all right. The Red Brick Road; we'll follow it."

"Well let's get going Honus." Rooster said. "How far are we going to go?" He asked

"It's not far at all," the Blue Witch lied. "It's one of the more pleasant paths around." She lied again. "And it's a direct path there so you can't get lost," she added a third lie just to keep things even.

"Where's the yellow road lead?" Honus asked. "Now that I think about it, we were on a blue road back at that circle."

"The yellow road is closed for repairs; they're adding curbs or rumble strips or something. And the blue road has lots of dead ends at places that don't have what you need; the Witch of the South's talisman." The Blue Witch gripped her wand tightly. "Why don't' we just leave that road for another time?" She said sweetly. "If reviews are good, we can discuss that road next time. How's that?" Her thoughts went to a particularly annoying candy maker. "It'll be a scrump-dilli-umtious reunion."

"Okay," Honus said, not understanding. "Do I need any supplies or anything? Usually before taking a trip, you need supplies and such. Like maybe a bedroll and some food." He thought back to his own backpack under his bed- he had put together a week's provisions, a bedroll, extra clothes, as well as some money to buy any extra items as the need arose. "Or maybe some money?"

"You'll find all you need along the road," The Blue Witch said. "Folks are always friendly around here," she lied again since she was on a roll.

"Right," the Mayor said, stretching the conversation out to grab another song. "It's a lot like if you come down to the river. Bet you gonna find some people who live." He snapped his fingers. "You don't have to worry 'cause you got no money..."

"People by the river are happy to give!" The little people all sang. "Down by the big wheel that keeps turning."

"Turning?" Rooster asked.

"Turning!" The people all sang.

"We will discuss the Chocolate River another time," The Blue Witch interrupted.

"Only if there are reviews?" Honus asked.

"Yes; only then." The Blue Witch answered truthfully. Ending her three-week streak.

"Alright-ee then," the Mayor said, wanting not only the strange young man and his actually fairly normal rooster to leave, but also the Blue Witch. Especially the Blue Witch. "Off with you young man. Follow the red brick road, like the good wit... err like she said."

Honus nodded. "Okay." He looked down at the spiral and stepped onto the very center of it. He walked in a tight circle as the red spiraled out. "Follow the Red Brick Road," he said as he moved along the tight spiral.

"You can just start going in that direction to the edge of town," the Blue Witch said as she pointed over her shoulder. "It's not like you'll lose the path between here and there. Honestly."

"Tra-la-la-la. La-la-la, la-la-la!" Rooster said.

All the townsfolk replied in kind.

The Blue Witch sighed. "I'm beginning to worry about this place called Kansas. And their public education system."

Honus moved along the red bricks, looking down as he went. "Thank you for your help, Ma'am." He said as he walked off, Rooster close behind.

The Blue Witch let her hands drop to her sides, wand clattering against the colored road. "The things I go through."

"You know, we had several of the guilds here who could have said something encouraging," the Mayor said. "In song even."

"Next time, perhaps," the Blue Witch said. "When our next Kansas dolt arrives."

"Promise?" The Mayor said hopefully. "Really?"

"I so solemnly swear to you Mayor of Munchkinland, Overseer of the Nexus," she answered, fully expecting the Mayor to not be in office by the time the next one showed up- after all, it had been a good ten years between the previous visitor and this one. "The guilds get to sing next time."

"Lollipop too?"

"Yes; even those hell-raising hooligans." The Blue Witch said.

"You know, if you don't mind me saying, the odds are that the Witch of the South is going to kill that kid before he has a chance to even get close to her magical star of power."

The Blue Witch nodded at the Mayor. "I do mind you saying, actually." She looked at the young man and rooster as they walked off. "And that's if he even gets to her castle."

"Want me to send a Lollipop Guild Enforcer to help him out?"

The Blue Witch smirked. "Well, well Prince Denis; maneuvering to keep your position of authority?"

The Mayor shrugged "Just trying to be helpful," he lied. "You want me to send one or not?"

The Blue Witch looked off to where Honus was walking. "I can't imagine your diminutive constituents being any sort of help outside of your city's boundaries," she remarked.

"That's where you're wrong. Those Lollipop Guilders might be little, Miss Blue, but you cross them and you'll be on the receiving end of a world-class, Teamster-style ass-kicking."

"You don't say." The Blue Witch said. She panned her wand in a large circle, conjuring a bubble. "Send one their way. I'll keep an eye on them as far as I can."

The mayor nodded. "Sure thing, Miss Blue." Things were looking up- with a Lollipop Guild Enforcer along for the trip, he was now certain that the talisman would come to him

49

instead of the Blue Witch. The rumors were that the Blue Witch was planning on eliminating the other three witches as well as The Wizard himself. The mayor shuddered at the thought of the Blue Witch ruling the lands unchecked and unchallenged. At least with the talisman, he could help the Witch of the East, whom he was on good terms with, to keep her power. Everything hinged on getting the talisman to her. If things went well, he would go from 'Prince Denis' to 'King Denis'. "You can count on me."

"I won't." The Blue Witch said as she completed the circle. A sphere of magical energy surrounded her and lifted her off the ground. "But I'll be in touch anyway." She said as she lifted off.

Mayor Denis turned around. "I need a volunteer from the Lollipop Guild."

No one made eye-contact with him. Two small people ducked back under the flowers they were beside. Since they had large flowers on their heads, they blended in nicely. Another just lay down and went to sleep.

"It's to get the talisman from the Witch of the South and get it to the Witch of the East before the Blue Bombshell gets her hands on it."

For what it was worth, the Witch of the East was at least fun at parties and unlike the one in the South, did not turn her nose up at a bar-b-ques. The last summer solstice festival lasted late into the night thanks to the Witch of the East's fireworks displays. Plus, she had brought a dozen barrels of green beer, carried by her (also very fun to party with) flying monkeys. The Witch of the East was the way to go when picking allies. And partying.

"Anyone? We need to keep the Witch of the East in power. Or at least in control of her own lands."

Three very little, colorfully dressed men stepped forward.

"What'cha need from the Lollipop Guild?" Asked a stout little man with bright orange hair. "Local one oh eight of..."

"The Lollipop Guild." Finished the second as he tucked his thumbs behind his suspenders.

"Yeah, the Lollipop Guild," reiterated the third out of the corner of his mouth as he kicked a foot out.

Mayor Denis looked at the trio. "Ahh, our esteemed, elected in perpetuity Shop Stewards." Calling them 'enforcers' was something someone did when they weren't around. "Well, if you could possibly help that wayward youth from Kansas with his errand, we would all appreciate it," he said nervously. He jerked a thumb over his shoulder. "Just to make sure that he makes it there okay and gets that talisman from the Witch of the South."

The three moved forward, crowding Mayor Denis.

"It in our statement of work?" One Shop (Enforcer) Steward asked.

"Well..." Began the mayor. Truth be told, long-term escort duty was not covered under the union bylaws. Escorts by the hour were another matter entirely; they were covered by the petty cash fund.

"Off the books work is fine. We'll do blackleg work if we needs to," said another Shop (Enforcer) Steward out of the side of his mouth.

The third kept his thumbs hooked in his suspenders and just gave an easily-denied-at-an-indictment wink.

"We can work something out if need be," said the second.

"Well, I'm not really sure what this job entails. But I really don't want a full-fledged negotiation if at all possible." The Mayor said.

51

"You want him to not make it back?" Asked the one out of the side of his mouth. Thanks to an altercation with the Confectioners Combine, one side of his mouth was now permanently scarred and turned down into a frown.

"Well, to be honest, all I really care about is the talisman."

"Ya got it, Mayor," said the one with his thumbs hooked around his suspenders. "We'll take care of it for ya." He winked. "And that's all ya needs to know."

"Well, tha...thank you for that." Mayor Denis wiped his brow. "I think with all this excitement, I might just go take a nap under my topiary over at the Blue Roundabout."

Ned stifled a chuckle.

"Yeah. Ya go do that, Mayor. We got's dis." Said Yellow Hair. "We'll take care of it oh so discretely."

"And eliminate that Kansas kid oh so neatly." Said Thumbs-Around-Suspenders.

"Really?" Mayor Denis said, surprised. 'Neat' wasn't usually how the Enforcers worked. Flipped wagons, fires, and broken legs were how they usually left their mark.

"Well, it's more a sayin' than anythin' else," said Yellow Hair. "T' be honest wit ya, it's probably going to be messy."

"Well, we'll just leave it at that." With a wave, the Mayor loped off, hoping for a nice quiet nap under his own likeness.

It wasn't to be.

~~~~~~~~~~~~~~~~~~~~~~~~~~~~

Rooster glanced at Honus.

"Follow, follow, follow, follow. Follow the Red Brick Road."

Rooster looked at Honus.

"Follow, follow, follow the Red Brick road."

Rooster stared at Honus.

"Follow the Red Brick... Follow the Red Brick..." Honus looked down at Rooster. "Follow the Red Brick Road."

Rooster shook his head.

"Ohhhh we're off to see the Witch. The evil Witch of the South. If ever there was an evil witch, the Witch of the South is one. Because... Because... Because....Because of all the terrible..."

"If you keep singing that song, I'm going to kill you right out here in the open."

"Sorry," Honus said. "It's kind of catchy. You know?"

"Oh yeah, I know. It's catching me right between the eyes."

The pair walked in silence for a while.

"I think we should have brought food with us."

"Yeah." Honus nodded at Rooster. "That nice lady did rush us out of town back there."

Rooster did a double-take. "Nice? You think she was *nice*?"

"Well, sure. You don't get to wear all that lace and not be nice."

"So I'm the straight man. Got it."

"You're a Rooster," Honus reminded.

Rooster sighed. "I need a better agent." He ruffled his feathers. "These self-published gigs are rough."

"What?"

"Nothing. You hungry?" Rooster asked, changing the subject.

"I am, actually. I had just sat down to dinner when I... Uhhh."

"You uhh-ed at the table? Bad manners, that."

"No; I ended up here."

"I see. What were you eating?"

Honus scrunched up his face. "Watery vegetable stew."

"Stew, by definition is a mixture of meat and vegetables cooked in a liquid, typically thickened with flour." Rooster said. "Sounds to me like you were eating soup."

"Yeah. They call it stew though."

"It's not. If those editors were worth anything, they'd go back and swap that stew for soup back at the beginning."

"What?"

"Nothing. Probably won't happen anyway. It'll stay stew."

"There's no meat in it either." Honus said.

"Got something against meat?"

The pair crested a hill and started down into a bright, grove-filled valley.

"Not me," Honus said. "But Miss Devinell does not approve of meat."

"She some sort of religious nut?"

"I don't think so."

"Well I'm a fan of it," Rooster said. He took two quick hops to the edge of the road and pecked at a bright green grasshopper.

"Hey, hey! Can we talk this over?" The grasshopper squeaked as it flailed.

Rooster tipped his beak at the sky and swallowed the grasshopper whole. He looked at Honus, "You say something?"

Honus shook his head. "I think it was the grasshopper."

"I see. I wondered why you wanted to discuss my snack."

"Don't you think it's odd that grasshoppers talk."

"No, why?" Rooster hopped back to the side of the road and grabbed another grasshopper. Before it could argue for its release, he ate it as well.

"Where I come from, grasshoppers don't talk." Honus hesitated. "Neither do chickens." He looked across valley and spotted a herd of cows. "Or cows."

"Well, cows would be absurd, so I'm with you on that. It's a good thing that I'm a rooster not a chicken then."

"No; *no* animals don't talk. Well, I saw a parrot that talked at a county fair once, but that's it."

"If you only have one rule to live by, it should be 'never trust a talking carnie parrot'."

"Okay."

"So, no talking animals or meat. No wonder you left."

Honus shook his head. "I didn't so much as leave as I was taken here. And I eat meat. Fish, beef, lamb, chicke..." His voice trailed off.

"Okay then." Rooster cocked his head up at the boy. "What was that last one?"

"Hey, apples!" Honus said as he pointed. "You eat apples?"

"Not unless I have to. But I'll eat any worms you find in them. Did you just say you eat chickens?"

"I like apples," Honus said, keeping to his new conversation. "Either plain or as pies. And that nice lady said there would be stuff found along the way." He moved to the edge of the road. "Let's pick a couple."

Rooster shook his head. "Fine, let's grab a couple of apples for you. I'll keep my eye out for grasshoppers. But I get any worms you find."

"That's not a problem." Honus moved toward an apple tree.

The tree stood there.

Honus slowed down.

The tree remained reticent.

Honus stopped in front of the tree, appraising it.

"Something wrong?" Rooster said. He hopped into the tall grass and started looking for more grasshoppers. "Thought you were hungry."

"Well, being hungry makes me want to take an apple. Recent events make me want to be cautious about it."

"What harm could there be in taking an apple?" Rooster asked as he pecked at a Cricket that hopped deftly to the side.

"You never know."

"See?" Honus said as he pointed at the tree. "That sounded like a threat."

"Well, as far as threats go," the Apple Tree said. "That was pretty mild."

"Can I have an apple or two?" Honus asked.

The Apple Tree appraised him. "Hmmm." It said.

Rooster pounced on the Cricket.

"Hold on now!!" The Cricket squeaked. "I'm on my way to work! Got a job to do- a little boy's counting on..."

Honus and the Apple Tree turned to look at Rooster who was holding a large cricket in his beak.

The Cricket adjusted his top had with one leg and shook the tiny umbrella he was holding in another at Rooster. "You need to let me go!"

"Truthfully, in good conscience, I can't let a tasty meal get away," Rooster said out of the side of his beak."

"Well, always let your conscience be your guide," the Cricket said matter-of-factly. "Oh- wait!"

Rooster tipped his head back and swallowed the insect. "I think I'm going to peck them to death first from now on; it's getting disturbing, negotiating with one's food."

"That's reasonable, I suppose."

Honus nodded at the tree. "Well, I'd prefer to just ask for a couple of apples than to do anything that drastic."

The tree shuddered, sending several apples to the ground. "There ya go, sonny. Thanks for asking. Nothing's more annoying than just getting picked by a stranger. Stealing's what it is, frankly."

Honus bent over and picked up the apples- four in all. He put two in one pocket and a third in his other pocket. The last he polished on his vest. "Thank you, Mister Tree."

The Apple Tree put two of its lower limbs on its trunk. "Mister?"

"Well, I... I'm not a very good judge of trees. Miss?" he tried.

"Missus." The Apple Tree gestured across the street. "Been married for over twenty years now. To a Granny Smith across the road."

"Sexy," Rooster said.

"What?" Honus asked.

"I'll explain it to you when you're older," Rooster said. He winked at the Apple Tree. "Good for you, Missus Tree and don't let anyone tell you otherwise." Rooster hopped back to the road. "Back on the Red Brick Road." He pointed with his wing.

"Oh dear, that's what you're following?" Apple Tree said to Honus.

"What?" Honus asked.

"The Red Brick Road, remember?" Rooster said. He pointed at the road. "We got places to go. Thanks for the apples." Rooster flapped a wing as Honus, "Say thanks for the apples."

"Thanks for the apples," a confused Honus said as he walked to Rooster.

"You boys keep away from the s'Mores; stick to the road," Missus Apple Tree said. "Oh dear. Best of luck."

"Beware the Magpies," A Pear Tree said. "Now go."

"Thanks?" Honus said as he started to walk.

When the pair got farther away the Pear Tree remarked: "They'll probably be safe on the road."

"Someone should go with them," Missus Apple Tree said.

"No one brought them here," an old Apple Tree -a Braeburn-snapped. "No one wanted them here."

"We should have told them," Missus Apple Tree said.

"Are you kidding?" The Pear Tree said. "What do you think they would say? They'd say we were soft in the trunk."

"Well... they'll be okay." Missus Apple Tree said, not entirely convinced.

~~~~~~~~~~~~~~~~~~~~~~~~~~

Honus and Rooster continued through the small valley, Honus eating two of the apples, and Rooster eating a half dozen more insects. As they went, the trees got closer and closer to the road until they were walking in a forest.

"What happened to the fruit trees?" Rooster asked.

"What's a smore?"

"I have no idea. What's a magpie?"

Honus looked down at Rooster. "A Magpie is a kind of bird of course. How do you not know that; you're a bird?"

Rooster flapped his wings angrily. "Well, do you know every kind of Human?"

Honus considered that for a moment. "I suppose not."

As the pair rounded a corner, they came to a fork in the road.

"Huh." Honus said.

"You're getting a better handle on that." Rooster said.

"Thanks."

The pair stopped and stared at the Red Brick Road as it veered off in two directions.

"I don't believe this was mentioned by that woman who may not have been as nice as she first seemed."

"You're also becoming a better judge of character."

Honus looked down at Rooster. "I don't really trust you all that much."

Rooster nodded. "Yeah, you're getting good at character judging."

They looked at the fork for a little longer.

"Which way should we go?" Honus asked.

"Given a choice, I'd go down the path that gets us out of this forest."

"That would be best." Honus took a few steps down one path. "How about we go down this one for a while and if it doesn't seem to be going in the right direction, we come back and go down the other path for a while."

"What, and keep doing that until we die of old age?"

"Do you have a better..."

A long howl interrupted Honus.

"I've got a bad feeling about this," Rooster said.

They both looked in the direction to the howl.

"Do you have any idea how far away..."

Another howl, this time from the opposite direction interrupted Honus.

"Okay, I say we pick a path and go down it." Rooster said, he moved up beside Honus. "This one seems as good as any. What does a smore look like, anyway?"

"I don't know what one is so there's no way I would know what..."

A third howl- this time from behind them interrupted Honus.

"Maybe you should just stop talking," Rooster suggested. "Seems you're attracting them."

Honus nodded. He pointed down the path they had started down.

"Works for me." Rooster said.

"Alright then. Let's get..."

Three howls pealed through the forest. They seemed surrounded.

"If you would make an effort to *not* pick me up by my neck when you make a run for it, I'd appreciate it."

Honus scooped up Rooster and took off at a run down the left Red Brick Road.

After a minute, Rooster craned his neck to look around Honus' arm. "Are you sure you're running as fast as you can?"

"I'm running to keep running for as long as possible," Honus said as he breathed hard. "If I made a sprint for it, I'd have been..."

The howls seemed to be closer this time.

"Less talking, more deep breathing."

Honus skidded to a stop. The path forked again.

"Now this is getting annoying." Rooster said. "Which way now?"

"Some folks go that way." A voice said.

"Did you say something?" Rooster craned his neck up at Honus.

"And other folks go that other way."

Honus shook his head. "No; that wasn't me." Honus looked around the forest. He saw trees of various -mostly unnatural-colors, a small dilapidated picket fence and a ramshackle house. It looked as if the forest had grown around and through a small homestead decades ago. "There's a house over there, maybe there's someone there who can help." He started to walk toward the leaned-over, little house.

"I don't think that's such a good idea." Another voice said. Right behind Honus.

Rooster jumped up onto Honus' head. "Behind you!"

Honus turned quickly. There was no one there. He looked down. There was a very colorfully dressed little person standing there. Between his blue and red checkered pants, and yellow plaid shirt and green seersucker vest, he looked like he had dressed in complete darkness. In a thrift store that was run by color blind circus clowns. In stark contrast to the jovial outfit, he was holding a large (to scale) and menacing looking pipe wrench. Honus took a step back to put some space between himself and the interloper. "Hello there, Sir," He tried.

"Hello back at you," The little man said. "I'm supposed to be helpin' ya out."

"Out of where?" Rooster said.

"Here, 'course." The little man said. "You seem to be in a pinch."

"Don't you want my help instead?" A voice said.

Honus, Rooster, and the little man turned to look at the little house.

"No, we don't need yer help, *brainless*." The little man snapped. He pointed at the far end of the house with the pipe wrench. "Far side." A scarecrow was on a pole there. He had his arms crossed, pointing in opposite directions. "Steer clear of them things."

"Why's that?" Honus took a step toward the homestead. "Scarecrows aren't anything to be afraid of."

"Crows are scared of them," Rooster said. "And they're pretty bright birds, crows. Maybe they know something we don't."

"Just get me down from this pole and we can talk this over," the Scarecrow said. He tried to reach over his shoulder. "I'm not sure about a lot of things, but if you just turn this bent nail..."

"No way, hay-man." The little man said. He looked up as Honus. "There's a whole crop of them talking scarecrows out and about, causing mischief and mayhem. Bad incantation or something."

"Those are falsehoods," the Scarecrow said to Honus. He let his arms drop to his sides. "Started by folks that don't know any better."

"It's best to leave him right there. He was put there for a reason."

The Scarecrow swiveled his head to the little man. "Loan me that pipe wrench for a moment."

"There's even less of a chance of that, cow-food." The little man tightened his grip on the pipe wrench. "Let's get going. I'm telling you, he was stuck there for a reason."

The scarecrow stared at the little man for a long moment. Finally, he tilted his head back and shouted: "THEY'RE OVER HERE! AAAAOOOOOO!"

"I say we listen to the little guy." Rooster said.

"Stop that!" Honus said. "Maybe we should just let him down."

"AAAAOOOOO!" Howled the Scarecrow.

"Let's get moving," the little man said. He pointed down the Red Brick Road. "That way."

"But we're lost," Honus said. "There's all these forks and we don't know which to take."

"AAAAOOOOO! COME GET THEM! AND GIVE ME THEIR BRAAAINS!"

"What?" Honus said. "Our what?"

"Listen to the little guy!" Rooster said again. "I like my brains right where they are!"

"The path splits up and wanders but it all ends up coming together as long as you don't double back." The little man started down the fork on the right side. "No matter what, we need out of here before them things get t'us because we can't bed down in the forest."

Honus looked back at the Scarecrow. "Sorry, Mister Scarecrow; I think you need to just stay there."

"I'm going to knock the stuffings out of you and make them into a tie! AAAOOOOOO!" Now the Scarecrow pointed at them. "Over here! KALIDAHS, HO!"

Several howls rang through the forest from various directions.

"Catch up to that little guy!" Rooster hopped up and down on Honus' head. "Go already!"

Honus turned and started to run after the little man who was now a good thirty yards ahead. As he ran he reached up and cradled Rooster in the crook of his arm with his head by his elbow. "Keep an eye out behind us!"

Rooster stuck out his head and looked back. "So far so... Huh."

"What?" Honus started to look back.

"Do NOT look back. Trust me on that. Just keep running as fast as you can and if you pass that little guy, just keep going. Maybe he'll slow them down."

"What do they look like?" Honus said as he ran. "How many of them are there?"

"One that I can see. No wait, three. Well that's much better."

"How is three better than one?"

"I thought it was one really big one with three heads. Seems it's just three smaller ones."

"When you say smaller..."

"Small like a Grizzly Bear. Or maybe a Black Bear."

"I was hoping small like a raccoon."

"Not even close."

"What do they look like?"

"Teeth. Lots of teeth. Claws on the ends of all four legs." Rooster tilted his head to the side. "Gads."

"What?" Honus started to look.

"Don't do it!" Rooster said. "You'll be scared stiff and we'd be goners for sure. Just run." He kept looking back. "If I were a chicken, I'd crap an egg about now."

"How about a hint?"

"Bears, and Tigers, and Badgers." Rooster said.

"Oh my." Honus said.

"Or something else with long claws."

He took several deep breaths and picked up his pace. He finally caught up with the little man and slowed to match his pace. "How far do we have to run? Those things are chasing us."

"They'll chase us until we either stop running or we are out of the forest."

"Are they gaining on us, Rooster?"

"No, they're keeping their distance. Just keep running."

"Told ya," the little man said. "As long as we keep moving, we're safe. As soon as you stand still, they'll pounce on you."

"Then what?" Honus said.

The little man looked up at Honus. "It'll be lunch time."

"Well, I don't mind that you mentioned that," Rooster said, "because I could use another couple of crickets. Oh, wait. You mean for them, don't you." He craned his neck out to look back. "Just keep moving, Honus."

The little man slowed down.

"Don't slow down, Honus," Rooster said again. "No hard feelings, little guy, but there's no way I want to deal with those things. Maybe if they eat you, we'll make it out."

Honus slowed to keep with the man. "We'll stick together."

66

"Bad idea. Really bad idea," Roster said. "What we need... Huh"

After Rooster didn't finish his sentence, Honus shook him. "What do we need?"

"They slowed down when we did. Not as much as we did, so they're getting closer, but they definitely slowed down."

"As long as your feet are moving, you're safe from them." The little man slowed to a walk. "Just keep looking forward and keep moving."

Honus slowed to match the little man's pace again. "Are you sure?"

The little man nodded. "They'll chase you until you stop." He looked over at Honus. "Hey, you chicken; stop lookin' at them!"

"I'm a Rooster, for your information." Rooster said. He was still looking back.

"Stop looking at them no matter what you are." The little man said. "That annoys them. Just look ahead." He pointed with his pipe wrench.

Honus turned Rooster in his arm so his head was at his chest. "Do what he says, Rooster."

"Smart boy." The little man lifted the pipe wrench and put it across his shoulders, hands draped down on both ends. "We've only got about ten minutes then we'll be clear of the forest and then we can stop."

"Thank you, Sir."

"Marren," said the little man. "Stop calling me 'sir'."

"Okay, Marren," Honus said. He patted Rooster's head. "This is Rooster."

"Do *not* pat my head."

"Figured as much." Marren said. He slowed even more to a casual walk.

Honus slowed to match him.

"What are you doing?" Rooster said. He pecked at Honus. "Just keep your pace. That Marren's got a death wish or something."

Marren shook his head. "It's common knowledge." He turned and glanced at Honus and Rooster. "For locals anyway, that Kalidahs only attack when you try to turn and fight them or just stand your ground. Just walk away nice and peaceful like and they'll let you be."

Honus did a little jump. "Hey!" He reached up and swatted at his neck.

"What?" Rooster started to look behind Honus then stopped. "What is it?"

"It's breathing down my neck!"

"Typical. Just ignore it. They're trying to trick you into looking back." He shrugged. "Or stopping. I don't recommend either."

"I have to say the hot breath is really not very nice," Honus said. He ducked his head. "Is ducking okay?"

"Should be fine. There's only one way to be sure with Kalidahs."

"Ya dropped something." One of the Kalidahs said. "Looks important. Some sort of legal document, methinks."

"Don't fall for it," Marren warned. "That's a classic ruse."

"What's the only way to be sure with Kalidahs?" Rooster asked.

"You try it and if you get eaten, then it wasn't a good idea." Marren said.

Honus stood up straight and tried not to cringe as the largest creature loomed over him.

"Somethin' jus' fell from yer pocket," the largest of the Kalidahs said. "T'was shiny."

"How much farther?" Honus asked.

"Got a light?" Another Kalidahs tried. "I really need me a smoke."

Marren took his pipe wrench off his shoulder and pointed with it. "We only need to go up that rise and around the bend then we'll be out of their territory. We'll be in Quadling Country then and they can't follow us there."

"Why not?" Rooster asked.

"Quadling Country isn't zoned for Kalidahs, of course."

"Can't get a variance," one of the smaller Kalidahs admitted. "Unless you'll sign this petition. Want to sign the petition?"

"We've submitted for it sever'l times. Not much good without a petition," said another. "Oooh, ya dropped yer pen. It's right behind ya."

"And smores?" Honus asked.

Marren jerked a thumb over his shoulder. "That's that area back there where we took the left fork instead of the right one. Dangerous beasts, s'Mores. Foul critters they are. The area is named for them there are so many of them there. We definitely want to avoid that place."

"But we went right." Rooster said.

"Did we?" Marren started to look back then caught himself. "Huh."

"What are we running into?"

"s'Mores Country, of course." Marren said. "Which is really kind of a problem."

Honus' hair tussled as the Kalidah sniffed his head deeply. "How can that be worse than this?" He said as he ducked.

"Well, as it was explained to me, S'mores only attack people who are moving. You need to stand perfectly still until they get bored or look the other way, then you move real quick until they look at you again. It's like that kid's game Red Light - Green Light. Except it's your life on the line."

"And the level of absurdity just hit new peaks," Rooster said. "We've got monstrous Kalidahs behind us that we can keep at bay by moving and..." He cocked his head to the side. "Are S'mores monstrous or more your size, Marren?"

"They tend to eat Kalidahs." Marren said.

"Of course they do. Thanks for the clarification," Rooster said. "So monstrous behind us that will eat us if we stop, and bigger monstrous in front of us that only eat us if we move. So, what do we do?"

"Hope for a commercial break to solve the issue off screen?" Marren suggested.

"A what?" Honus asked.

"My agent and I are really going to have a long talk about the gigs he gets me," Rooster said. He cocked his head to the side. "Then we just need the left path then, right? As long as we don't encounter any s'Mores you know we could just..."

A loud scream pealed through the air.

The Kalidahs all stopped.

70

"Nice; and you didn't even have to ask what a s'More sounded like," Marren said. "See? These self-published gigs aren't all bad. What were you getting at, Rooster?"

"If those things behind us won't attack as long as we're moving, let's just walk in a nice big arc and head back the other way and take that left path you so cleverly missed."

"There's an insult in there, I think." Marren said.

"You're an idiot who's most likely going to get us killed." Rooster said flatly.

"There is it."

"Okay, so a nice gradual turn then." Honus pointed to his right. "We'll do a nice wide turn going from right to left. Everyone ready?"

"I'm along for the ride," Rooster said.

"I'll follow you," Marren said. "Lead the way."

With a nod, Honus veered slowly to the right edge of the path. He walked casually in a broad left arc in front of two massive S'mores and then to the left edge of the path. When he got there, he meandered back to the middle of the path, heading in the opposite direction. "Did anyone else notice the two large, lionish-buffaloish looking statues there in the path?"

"All I saw was a couple of s'Mores," Marren said.

"Oh hell." Rooster said.

The three Kalidahs started to drool as the trio walked directly toward them.

"When did they stop following us?" Rooster said.

"About the time those s'Mores showed up, I imagine," Marren said. "Kalidahs are ravenous but they aren't stupid." Marren stopped walking. "Stop walking, kid."

71

Honus came to a stop barely ten feet from the group of Kalidahs.

"You look tasty," a Kalidahs remarked. He ran his tongue across sharp teeth.

"I'm not," Honus said. "Honest I'm not."

"Me neither." Rooster said.

"Aren't you a white meat?" The larger of the three Kalidahs asked. "You're right up there with pork, I think."

"You got me confused with someone else." Rooster craned his neck around. The two s'Mores were looking back and forth. "Can't they see us?"

"They might not be able to," Honus said. "Maybe that's why standing still keeps them from eating you."

"Pretty sure you're one of them edible meats," a Kalidahs said as he eyed Rooster.

"Ooh," Rooster whispered to Honus. "Get ready. Get ready."

"Just stand still so they can't see us," Honus said.

"But *we* can see you," the third Kalidahs said. He ran a tongue along one side of his mouth, over his nose and down the other side. "Now you want to push our buttons by standin' there in front of us? Darin' us to eat youse? Rude is what that is."

"I'm fairly certain you're that white meat folks talk about," the first Kalidahs said.

"Get ready."

The largest Kalidahs smirked. "Keep standin' still so we eat ya. But if you move, then you have to deal with the..."

"Go now! GO!" Rooster said as he flapped his wings.

Honus bolted in between two of the Kalidahs. When he got to the other side, he spun around.

The pair of Kalidahs were still facing the s'Mores. And Marren.

"What was that?" Marren said. "You're just going to leave me?"

"No hard feelings, little plumber." Rooster said. "Let's go Honus, back the way we came then down the path to the right. We're on our way."

"Why you!" Marren brought his pipe wrench down and gripped it tightly by the handle. "I'm going to bash your head in!"

"We're not going to leave you Mister Marren," Honus said.

The three Kalidahs took a quick step forward as the S'mores both looked into the forest.

"We're gonna eat you first, like the little Munchkin snack that you is." The largest Kalidahs said.

"You, then your little friends too," said a second.

Rooster hopped out of Honus' arms and flapped his wings as he hit the ground. "Hey you s'Mores! Come and get some nice tasty white meat!" He strutted back and forth.

"Tol' ya he was white meat," the smaller Kalidahs told the largest one. "Says he's tasty as well."

"Rude that is; lyin' to folks that plan on eatin' ya."

The pair of s'Mores lowered their massive lion heads and stalked forward. Toward the Kalidah's.

"Now jus' a minute there, Mister Chicken," the largest Kalidahs said. "How 'bout we work something out."

Rooster stopped moving. "Like what?"

73

The s'Mores returned to scanning the area looking for movement.

"Well, how 'bout we all call it even b'tween us?"

"You mean you don't eat us and I don't lure the s'Mores over to eat you?"

"I'm still hoping for a scene break then a jump," Marren admitted.

"Well, I was thinkin' more that we only eat one or two of youse." Admitted the larger Kalidahs.

Rooster flapped his wings. "Chic Chiri Chí!" He crowed.

The two s'Mores turned to look at him.

"Where you from?" A Kalidahs asked.

"Italy," Rooster replied.

"That explains it," it replied as it smirked. "Eye-talian chickens are the tastiest."

"Well, I'll have you know...Wait, what'd you say?" Rooster asked as he flapped his wings and eyed the large Kalidahs.

"Fine, fine. All three of youse gets t' go." Said the largest Kalidahs. "Now stop flappin' already!"

Rooster stood still.

"That's more like it."

"But how're we going to get Marren back?" Honus asked. "And get the Kalidahs away too."

"Now we got to get them away too?" Rooster said.

"Well, fair's fair, I think." Honus said. He looked at the s'Mores. "What a mess."

"Do we need them to look another way so everyone can get away?" Rooster asked.

"Yeah, dat would be nice," a Kalidahs said. "Opposite of rude even."

"Okay then." Rooster scooted to Honus. "Just throw me as far toward those s'More things as you can."

"What?" Honus shook his head. "How's that going to help?"

"Yeah, toss the white meat," said a Kalidahs.

Rooster ignored it. "If you toss me that way, I can fly over their heads and land behind them. Then I'll fly up into the trees to stay out of their reach, then I'll fly back over here."

"But chickens can't fly," Honus said.

"Ahhh...Toss him anyway."

Honus looked at the Kalidahs. "Keep out of this." He looked at Rooster. "Chickens can't fly."

"Well that's not actually true," Rooster said. "Fat chickens can't fly really far because they are fat. Skinny chickens can fly short distances to get to a roost or to get to food." He struck a dramatic pose. "As a sleek, well plumed Rooster, I'm able to manage some nice long flights."

"What's a long flight?"

"A good twenty feet. More if I'm up on something and flying down."

Honus shook his head. "I'm not too sure about this."

"Toss him already."

"Quiet you!" Honus picked up Rooster and turned around.

The s'Mores were almost to Marren.

"Come on scene break and jump," Marren said.

"Why didn't you say something?" Honus said. "Whose side are you on?"

"We're on our side," the largest Kalidahs said. "Figured while they ate the little guy we'd make a run for it."

"They're right behind me?" Marren fumed. He clenched his pipe wrench. "You stinking Kalidahses."

"I figured it would be 'Kalidahi'," Rooster said. "Go figure. Heave away, Honus." He stretched out his neck. "Make it a good throw."

Honus leaned back and lifted his leg, pausing for a moment before pivoting forward like he was throwing a Rooster fastball and side-armed the bird at the branch.

"Unusual form," a Kalidahs said as he watched Rooster's launch.

"Do what works," the other said.

"Finally!" Marren said as the scene changed.

~~~~~~~~~~~~~~~~~~~~~~~~~~~

The Blue Witch looked out at the countryside from her balcony. With a satisfied sigh, she took a bite of her freshly made scone.

"Bliss." She wiped the clotted cream on the corner of her mouth with a blue napkin. "That's what I have right now." She refused to look to the west and the roiling clouds and flashes of lightning that she knew in her heart were still there.

The hairs on the back of her neck stood up.

The Blue Witch took another bite of her scone.

She flattened the hairs on the back of her neck. "Breezy today." She tried as she took a sip of her Ozjeeling Tea.

The hairs on the back of her neck stood up again.

"Come on!" She pushed herself to her feet. "Just one restful moment, how is that too much to ask for?" She threw her cup over the side hoping it would hit someone on the ground, then stomped to the ornate door. She pushed through it and went straight to her Scrying Chamber. "How can you already be in trouble?" She asked as she stomped up the stairs on to the pedestal overlooking the map. She looked over the map-nothing seemed to be percolating more than normal. "You just started for goodness' sakes!" The Blue Witch whirled on the cauldron sitting on the platform. She gestured at it with both hands and it immediately began to boil. "I mean honestly."

The Blue Witch picked up a long-handled wooden spoon. She dipped it into the cauldron and swirled it around for a moment before lifting it out. The holes in the spoon allowed the bright blue fluid (bright blue was this year's green when it came to fluids) to drain back into the cauldron leaving behind a greyish mist. Pivoting around, she cast the mist over the map near The Nexus. "Now where are you?"

As the mist settled on the map, shadowy figures began to move about.

She dipped the spoon again in the cauldron and spread the mist farther along the Red Brick Road.

In the swirling mist she saw Honus standing in front of two s'Mores. Behind him were three Kalidahs (she was well aware that the plural and singular for the creatures was the same). "That's just absurd. What is that public education system in Kansas teaching its youth?"

As she spread more mist on the area, she could see a little person with Honus. She leaned over the railing to get a closer look at him. "Well, well; a handsome little Lollipop Guild Enforcer. One did come along after all." As she watched, Honus and the Rooster jumped back behind the Kalidahs, leaving the little man between them and the s'Mores. "Nicely done young man. Now off with your mission." She waved a hand to shoo Honus along.

The rooster strutted back and forth.

"What are you doing?"

As the Blue Witch watched, Honus picked up the rooster and prepared to throw him. "Chickens can't fly, you stupid boy."

As she shook her head, Honus tossed the rooster high toward the s'Mores. It was flapping furiously. And ineffectively.

"I see what you're doing. All for that delicious looking Lollipop Guilder that's probably going to kill you later on." The thought made her want the little man even more. As the rooster started to lose altitude, the Blue Witch reached out with the wooden spoon and lifted up on the mist-covered rooster. "Up a little more to reach that branch." She repeated the motion two more times to help the rooster reach the closest branch. "That stupid bird is going to think it can do that all the time." With a head shake, she leaned back to watch. "Now let's see what happens."

~~~~~~~~~~~~~~~~~~~~~~~~~~~

Marren looked around. The situation was exactly the same. "Munchkin nuts; that was no jump at all."

Rooster flared out his wings when he was at the apex of the arch and flapped hard. He kept his altitude for four or five flaps then started to descend. Right on top of the s'Mores.

The s'Mores opened their mouths, expectedly.

"That tasty little white meat won't make it."

"Fly, Rooster, fly!" Honus encouraged him.

Rooster gained several feet as if an unseen hand lifted him higher.

"Whoo hoo!" Rooster said as he flapped furiously. "Swifter than eagles!"

Marren leaned back and threw his pipe wrench at the s'Mores then ran between the Kalidahs to Honus.

The pipe wrench hit one of the s'Mores on the shoulder. Making it look away from Rooster.

"We ought to go," said the larger Kalidahs. "See yas back at the tree."

With nods from the other two, they sidestepped off the Red Brick Road and into the forest.

"I'm flying!" Rooster said. As he started to lose altitude again. "Look at me go!"

"Higher, Rooster. Higher!"

The s'Mores all backed up as Rooster passed over their heads.

Rooster inexplicably gained altitude again. "Like the mighty Condor, I soar!"

"Over here!" Honus raised his arms and waved them.

The s'Mores turned to look at Honus.

"You sure about this?" Marren asked.

"Not really."

"Stupid rooster." Marren started waving his arms as well. "Figured I'd go out like this."

"You thought you'd get eaten by s'Mores while tryin to save a flying rooster?"

"The details were kind of hazy, but yeah, seems about right."

"Head for the trees, Rooster!" Honus called.

With a final push, Rooster made it to the lowest branch of a tree. He looked down at the s'Mores. "Hah!"

The s'Mores looked up at Rooster then leaned in and had a quiet conversation.

"We should get out of sight," Marren said. "While they're distracted."

"That's a good idea." Honus said as he took a step backwards.

The s'Mores both turned to look at Honus and Marren. One licked its lips.

"Well nuts." Marren said. "Oh well; can't win 'em all." With that, he bolted down the

path.

"Run, Honus, run!" Rooster called. He flapped his wings. "Tasty white meat right here!"

The s'Mores turned to look at Rooster.

Honus ran down the path after Marren.

"Ahh, success." Rooster said, satisfied with himself. He looked down at the s'Mores. "What do you say to that?"

The s'Mores looked at each other for a long moment.

"Fellas?" Rooster tried. "What're you thinking?"

"Say, where'd we see that Tin Man?" A s'More finally said.

"Over by that other path," said the other.

"Blue one?"

"Naw; that yellow one. Where they're putting in those rumble strips."

Rooster looked back and forth as they spoke.

"That's what I thought. He's got that axe, if I recall correctly."

"That he does, brother. That he does." The s'More looked at the trunk of the tree that Rooster was occupying.

"Let's talk this over, guys" Rooster tried.

"Be right back. Keep an eye on the flapping white meat." With that, one of the s'Mores marched off into the forest.

The other s'More looked up at Rooster. "How about you just come down and save us all a bit of trouble."

"Not likely." Rooster scanned the area. Thanks to the trees being close to the path, he could easily make it from branch to branch in the direction that Honus had gone. "I've got a better idea."

"You giving up? Gonna marinate yourself?"

Rooster spread his wings. "Time for another feat of flying grace!" Rooster bounced on the branch several times to get it going, then on an upswing, leapt off.

The s'More watched as Rooster flapped furiously to a nearby branch.

"Stop doin' that." One complained.

Rooster landed roughly on the branch then hung on tightly. When the branch stopped moving, Rooster stood rock still.

"Hey, where'd ya go?" The s'More looked from the branch Rooster was on to the original one. "Well now; that's just annoyin'." He started to scan the other trees.

When he was looking the other way, Rooster half-flew, half-jumped to a nearby branch.

The s'More turned to look where Rooster had been sitting- the branch was still wobbling. "When that axe gets here," he warned, "you'll be sorry."

Rooster stared straight ahead, breathing quietly. He swiveled an eye to look at the creature. When it looked the other way, he jumped without looking back away from the Red Brick Road into the underbrush. The bushes were way over his head when he landed. He stood still anyway.

"Hey! I heard that!" The s'More said. "You know it's not nice taking advantage of someone's disability."

Rooster quietly backed away. Resisting the urge to answer.

"How about jus' a hint?" The s'More tried again.

Rooster turned and moved quickly in the underbrush, parallel to the road. After a dozen or so yards, he turned sharply and headed straight to the road. As he burst out of the underbrush onto the road, he ran headlong into Honus. "Did you see that? Did you see that?" Rooster stood and strutted back and forth. "Like an Eagle. Like a majestic Condor. The Owl even."

"I saw," Honus smiled. "It was very impressive."

"I helped too," Marren said as he stepped back onto the path.

"What were you doing over there?" Rooster asked.

"Taking a wiz."

"I see. Nice pipe wrench chucking," Rooster said.

"I've had a bit of practice."

"Plumbers throw wrenches?" Rooster asked. "Didn't know that."

"I've never heard of that either," admitted Honus. "You use a pipe wrench like that a lot?"

Marren looked at the sky. "I've been advised by my lawyers to not make any statements concerning closed cases."

"Closed cases?" Honus said.

"Or open ones. Or pending ones even." Marren looked up the road. "Well, let's get going then."

"Huh." Rooster said.

"Right. But we need to make sure we go back and get on the right path." Honus said.

"Well, technically we're already on the Red Brick Road. Or at least a Red Brick Road." Honus said, "But if you say we need to..."

"Follow, follow, follow. Follow the Red Brick Road." Marren sing-songed as he pointed down the path and started to skip.

"Then we're off to see the Witch. The despicable Witch of the South." Honus started walking the way they had come.

"And if ever there was a despicable witch, the Witch of the South is one because, because, becaaaaause..."

"Stop it," Rooster said.

"Because of all the despicable things she does?" Honus asked.

"I'm warning you two," Rooster pointed at Marren then Honus. "There'll not be any singing while we walk."

"Not any at all?" Marren looked dejected. "I mean, if there's one thing we little folk like is singing a song."

"Still." Rooster said. "Not every occasion requires a song."

"What about the sun coming up?" Honus said as he stifled a laugh. "You roosters make a commotion each and every time that happens."

"That's different," Rooster said defensively.

"We didn't used to sing all the time you know."

"In that case, I'm sure it will be easy to go back to not doing it." Rooster said as he fell in step beside the other two."

"Even when the sun comes up?"

Rooster glanced at Honus. "You're not helping, you know."

"Last time we had someone visit from the Kansas, he got us to singing."

"He *forced* you to sing?"

The trio rounded the corner to where the other branch on the road was.

"It's more he discovered our hidden talent." Marren said. "He led us in a rousing number that stuck in our heads. Now we can't help it. Especially since you're from the Kansas as well."

"Well save those songs for the next person," Honus said.

"Will there be another along?"

"Sure, sure," Rooster lied. "They all want to come visit." He winked at Honus. "Then you can sing your little hearts out."

Marren nodded. "Okay, I'll do my best. So that way is the right way." He pointed down the Red Brick Road. "It's that way."

"You know, where I come from we have these things called signs that we have up on roads and especially intersections of roads that let you know which way is what."

"Sounds absurd." Marren said. "Let's ease on down the road."

"Ease on down the road?" Honus said, not familiar with the term.

"Yeah, ease on down, ease on down..."

"You're doing it again," Rooster said.

"Sorry. It kind of just happens." Marren started down the other Red Brick Road from the first, wrong Red Brick Road to the correct Red Brick Road. "Oh, as was mentioned earlier, the sun will be going down and we'll need a place to spend the night. Can't just sleep out on the road."

Honus frowned. "I knew we should have gotten some money from that Witch."

"Maybe we can build something to sleep in," offered Rooster. "Either of you able to build a coop?"

Marren stared down at Rooster.

"Nothing fancy, really. Just a couple of levels, and a nice yard to peck and scratch in. And of course, a sturdy roof to stand on at dawn."

Marren shook his head. "We won't be building a coop." He looked around. "You know, I think we're going to be close to that other road here shortly and there's a little woodcutter's cabin sitting there.

"Do you think the woodcutter will let us stay there for the night?" Honus asked.

"I don't see why not." Marren pointed at a small rise to their right. "I think if we go to that high ground right there, we could see it."

"She should have given us food as well." Honus said. "I mean, we aren't even near a river for people there to give us food."

The trio walked to the top of the small hill and looked around.

"I don't see anything." Rooster said. "I need a perch."

Marren pointed. "There's the top of it. See it Honus?"

Rooster hopped to Marren's shoulder. "Ahh, there is it. What a dump."

"I see it. It doesn't look that bad." Honus looked over to the side. "There's that other road you mentioned. It's gold bricks?"

"What?" Marren started down the hill. "Of course not; it's just painted like that. If they were really gold, the whole road would have been gone in a week."

The trio walked across the yellow brick road.

"It's a major thoroughfare," Marren remarked.

The trio walked across the Yellow Brick Road.

"Where's this road go?" Honus asked.

"It goes from my home town to the docks at the Chocolate River, the Great Hilltop Kingdom, and the Emerald City." Marren said as he pointed. "The shack should be over there, I think."

"It goes to all those places?"

"Well a branch of it does, yes."

"And there are no signs."

"Don't be stupid." Marren said.

"Those sound like neat places," Honus said.

"Well, we're not going there," Rooster said. "We're going to see that Witch, take that star thing..."

"By force if we need to," Marren added.

"Yes, what he said. Hopefully what he said." Rooster continued, "And then get home. And since I'm in charge, that's what we're going to do."

"Even so, they sound interesting."

"Maybe we can go there later. How's that?" Rooster conceded.

"If the reviews are good?" Honus asked.

The trio walked to the front door of the quaint cabin.

"Exactly," Rooster said. "Did I mention this place was a dump?"

The trio walked up to the ramshackle cabin.

"Should we knock?"

"I say we take it by force." Rooster said. "Imminent domain even."

Honus shook his head as he knocked. "Honestly, you need to be less pushy." When no one answered, he knocked louder.

"Maybe he's out." Marren said. "Is it locked?"

Honus lifted the latch and pushed the door open. He leaned his head in. "Hello?"

When no one answered, Rooster pushed between Honus' legs and marched into the cabin.

"What a dump." Rooster said. "I hereby lay claim to this dump of a cabin." He stomped a foot.

Honus stepped into the cabin. "It doesn't look like anyone has lived here in a long time." He looked back at Marren. "You sure a woodsman lives here?"

"That's what I've heard." Marren said. "I haven't seen him personally, if that's what you mean."

Rooster hopped onto the bed. Dust floated up as he bounced on it. "I think I'll take the bed."

Marren and Honus stared at Rooster.

"You two can sleep on the floor."

"You going to pitch him out, or am I?" Marren asked. "I really need me a new pipe wrench."

"I'll talk to him," Honus said. "Hey, Rooster, why don't you go see if anything is around the cabin while we clean it up some for you."

Rooster hopped off the bed. "Good idea. This place is a dump." He marched out the door.

"Just lock it." Marren said. "If nothing's eaten him by the morning, we'll take him along."

Honus laughed. "He's not that bad once you get to know him."

"Oh? You've known him long?"

"Just today."

"And?"

"I can't imagine anything would be willing to risk the belly ache."

Marren smirked. "Let's see if this woodsman has left any food behind. Check that closet." He moved to the cupboard and opened it. "Hmmm. What do you have?"

"Some cloths. Metal polish. Cans of oil." Honus closed the closet. "That's weird; there's no clothes in there. An axe handle. Did you find food?"

"There's some steel wool. An axe handle you say?"

"Weird," Honus said again. "Yeah, I guess he has a spare."

"There's some dried meat and a nice looking round of cheese."

"That's a relief." Honus sat on the bed. It squeaked loudly.

Marren turned. He was holding a large piece of dried meat. "This has been here a while." He gestured over his shoulder. "And once we've cut off the green part of that cheese we'll only have half left."

"That's better than nothing." Honus bounced on the bed making it squeak loudly. "No one's lived here for a year, I'd say. When did you last hear about this woodsman?"

"I don't know. It's been a while though. I just heard there was one living out here where the Red and Yellow roads come close together."

Someone pecked on the door.

"Don't let him in." Marren said. "It's more food for us that way."

The pecking got louder.

"He'll do that all night and make tomorrow miserable." Honus stood and walked to the door. He put his ear to it. "As long as he doesn't start..."

"Chic Chiri Chí!" Rooster crowed from outside the door

"Oh boy."

"Who is it?" Marren called.

"It's me!" Rooster said testily.

"Prove it! There's lot of roosters out there, I'm sure." Marren said as he smiled. "You don't sound familiar."

"Cock-a-doodle-doo!" Rooster crowed. "Did you understand that one better?"

89

Honus opened the door. "The second crow was the same as the first."

"No, it wasn't," Rooster said as he strutted into the room.

Marren quickly moved to the bed and sat on it.

Rooster squinted an eye at him. "They are completely different, of course. Listen." Rooster cleared his throat and tilted his head back. "Chic Chiri Chí!" He crowed loudly.

"Okay." Honus said.

"And now this time." Rooster tilted his head back again. "Cock-a-doodle-doo!" He crowed.

"Sounds the same to me." Marren said.

"They're two *completely* different languages!" Rooster scratched at the ground with a claw. "You people. It's a good thing I'm running this campaign."

Honus closed the door. "Anyway, did you find anything useful out there?"

Rooster shook his head. "Some guy was mumbling about a soiled can or something. Some sort of knight since he was wearing armor. Of course, it was all rusted so he couldn't have been a good knight, so I pecked at his foot then left."

"Soiled can? What's that?" Marren asked.

"I was afraid to get more details and wasn't going to sit around to try and get them out of old silver britches."

Honus opened his mouth to ask when Marren pointed at him. "Just let it go. We need to get to sleep so we can get going in the morning." He pointed at Rooster. "And I'm sure that one's going to have us up at daybreak."

"I don't see why." Rooster said. He cocked his head to the side. "What'd you find to eat?"

90

"Some dried meat and some sharp cheese."

"I'll pass on the cheese but I'll take a piece of meat or two."

Marren tore a long sliver of meat and tossed it to Rooster. "There ya go." He pulled a knife from his sock. "Cheese for you, young man?"

Honus nodded as he sat in a rocking chair. "Please."

Marren wiped the knife on his pant leg then sliced the remaining piece of dried meat in half. He leaned forward and offered it to Honus. "Get the cheese next."

Rooster pecked and clawed at the meat. "This is some dry meat."

Honus bit into his piece of meat and tore off a chunk. "Well, any food is good food when you're hungry." He reached out and took a large piece of crumbly cheese from Marren. "And it's always easier sleeping on a full belly."

"Very true," Marren said.

The trio ate the meat and cheese, chatting until the sun was down. Finally, they went to sleep- Honus and Marren on the bed and Rooster begrudgingly perched on the rocking chair.

~~~~~~~~~~~~~~~~~~~~~~~~~

"Maaaa!"

Marren opened an eye. "What was that?"

"Chic Chiri Chi!"

"That sounds like Rooster. Must mean the sun's up." Honus said.

"No, not that second one." Marren closed his eye

91

"Maaaa!"

"There, that one." Marren said. "Honestly, how many languages does that chicken speak?"

"Maaaa!"

"Chic Chiri Chí!"

Honus sat up. "There's no way we're getting more sleep with all that racket; we might as well get going."

"Starting this early, we should be able to reach the Witch's castle just after dark."

"Maaaa!"

"Cock-a-doodle-doo even!"

Honus swung his legs off the bed, lifting them up and over Maren who was sleeping with his head opposite him. "Is he changing his voice now?" He padded to the door and opened it.

A large wolf lunged at the open door.

Honus slammed the door shut.

"Don't open the door!" Rooster yelled.

"Now you tell me!" Honus yelled back.

The wolf clawed at the door.

"That's what I was saying earlier!" Rooster yelled.

"Maaaa!"

"No, I don't think he understood you either." Rooster said.

Marren sat up and looked at the roof. "Who's on the roof with you?"

The wolf stopped clawing at the door.

No one said anything for a long moment.

Marren hopped off the bed. "That's just annoying." He looked up again. "Who is on the roof with you?"

"Oh me? I thought you were talking to the goat."

"Let's sneak out the back and let the wolves have him," Marren said. He moved to the window. It was too high for him to see out. "Is the coast clear?"

Honus went to Marren and pushed open the window. Two wolves were looking at the roof of the cottage. "No; there are two more wolves out here."

"Hey, Rooster, how many wolves are outside?"

"All of them!" Rooster called back. "Don't tell me you let them *inside*!"

"No, you stupid bird!" Marren yelled. "We're trying to figure out how many wolves are out there!"

"Oh, okay." Rooster said.

No one said anything for a long moment- only the sound of snarling wolves broke the silence.

Until Marren screamed: "HOW MANY WOLVES ARE OUT THERE YOU STUPID CHICKEN!"

"Three. Keep your pants on; there are three of them." Rooster said.

"Maaaa?"

"Oh, right. Sorry; four. Four's the number."

"That stupid bird." Marren scooted across the room and pushed a chair to the window then hopped onto it. "Let me see."

Two of the wolves were sitting looking up- ostensibly at Rooster and the goat.

"I suppose the other two are on the other side of the house. We could just wait them out."

Honus shook his head at the little man. "No; we're in a real fix here. All the meat's gone, and we have no water."

"Cheese is gone too."

A thought occurred to Honus. A thought that would never have occurred to him back home. "Excuse me Mister Wolves," he called out the window.

One of the wolves turned to look at him. "What?" it asked.

"Do you think we could talk this over?"

"Talk what over?" The wolf asked. It looked back at the roof. "Seems prrrretty settled to me."

"You stupid wolf!" Rooster called down from the roof. "Go chase your tail or something!"

The wolf gestured at the roof with a paw. "Hear that? He's been doing that all morning. We're going to eat the little loudmouth."

"Well maybe we could..."

"You wouldn't know a good meal unless a cat pooped it!"

"Rooster!" Honus said loudly. "*Please* let me handle this."

"I still say we leave them," Marren said. "Seems their beef is with that rooster."

"Can we talk this over?" Honus tried again. "We're on an important job right now and we need that rooster to help out."

"Honestly, I can't imagine that rrrrooster helping with anything." The Wolf said matter-of-factly.

94

"I'm the leader of this group, you stupid dog!"

The wolf looked at Honus. He let one ear flop down as his head tilted to the side. "Rrreally?"

Honus shook his head.

So did Marren, who then pointed at his ear with a finger and twirled it around. With the other hand, he gestured at the roof.

The wolf nodded.

"They are both nodding, aren't they? They confirmed I am the one in charge!" Rooster said proudly. "Cock a doodle doo!" He crowed triumphantly.

"Grrrrreat." The wolf rolled his eyes. "Just great. What's this all-important job?"

"We're..." Honus looked down at Marren.

Marren shrugged. "I'd just tell him; if you can't trust a wolf, we've got bigger troubles."

"We're going to the Witch of the South to use her magical star to help us get back home." He said diplomatically- he wasn't sure whose side the wolves were on.

"If you get the chance to kill that witch while you're there, we'd appreciate it." The wolf said.

The other wolf growled. "Kill her really most sincerely dead."

"That's what I said!" Rooster called down.

"What's with the goat?" The wolf asked. It looked back up at the roof. "It with you as well?"

"We don't know anything about a goat." Honus said. "It's just me, this man, and the rooster."

"Maaaa!" The goat said loudly.

95

"The goat's with me," Rooster said. "I need a second in command."

"We're not taking some goat with us!" Marren said. "One stupid rooster is all the wildlife we can tolerate."

"She cooks," Rooster said. "Famous cook, this goat is."

The wolf ran its tongue along one side of its mouth, over its nose and across the other side. When it got there, it just hung down. "Tasty things, goats."

"Maaa!"

"We can't just leave it here to get eaten," Honus said quietly to Marren.

The wolf perked an ear toward the window.

"We don't owe that goat anything," Marren said.

The wolf nodded.

"Well, I'd feel bad just leaving it here to get eaten."

"Honus, listen to reason; the more in our group, the slower we'll go."

The wolf nodded.

"And," Marren continued, "what've you got against wolves anyway? They've got to eat, you know. This pack seems pretty reasonable to me."

The wolf drooled.

"This will be the last one." Honus said.

The wolf shook its head.

Marren sighed loudly. "A cooking goat?" His eyebrows went up. "Say, are you Gertrude?"

"Thaaat's me!" The goat said. "Heard of me, have ya?"

"Come on." Honus said. "You know this goat?"

The wolf lowered his head. "Crrrrud." He had heard of her as well.

"She a famous cook." Marren said. "Cooked for the Wizard, and high courts even."

"She ever cook for the Witch of the South?" Honus asked.

"I don't know. Probably though."

"You ever cook for the Witch of the South?" Honus asked loudly.

"Me? No." Rooster said. "Of course not."

Marren covered his face with his hands. "Not you, you stupid bird; the goat!" He clenched his fists. "Have you ever cooked for the Witch of the South!" He shouted.

"Sure I have." Gertrude answered.

The wolf scowled.

"Mister Wolf, if you could see yourself letting the goat come with us, we would appreciate it. Since she's been in the witch's castle, she can help us get in."

"What about the rooster?" The wolf cocked its head to the side. "Yerrr not gonna need him, rrright?"

"What rooster?" Marren asked. "We don't know anything about a rooster, right Honus?"

A smile came to the Wolf's face- long white teeth prominently displayed. "Now you're talking! Meat's back on the menu, boys!"

"We can't just leave him behind."

97

The Wolf's smile faded. His left ear drooped again. "Come on now."

"Honus is right!" Rooster said. "Without me you're leaderless! Foundering in a sea of despair even. Lost in a vast desert of unknowingness."

"It would serve your bellies well to not eat that gristly rooster," Marren said. "Sour stomachs for a week, I'd imagine."

"What?" Rooster said. He strutted back and forth on the peak of the roof. "Why I'll have you know I'd be the most tender and delicious meal they've had all.... errr." He scowled. "What I mean is..."

"Gads, just take that loudmouth and get out of our territory," the Wolf said as it stood. "Let's go find some nice quiet food someplace else."

With that the four wolves padded off.

But not without Rooster tossing at them: "Best decision you've made this week! That's like two *months* in dog years!"

"Rooster! Be quiet and get down here." Honus turned from the window and went to the door. "Let's get going, Marren. You said we could get to the castle by nightfall?"

Marren hopped off the chair. "If all goes smoothly and we keep to a good pace, we should be there right after nightfall."

"Don't even look back!" Rooster shouted at the wolves.

"Smoothly might be asking for too much," Honus said. He opened the door. "Let's go meet this famous goat."

~~~~~~~~~~~~~~~~~~~~~~~~~~

Honus and Marren walked around the side of the cottage.

"And that's when I learned I was lactose intolerant," Rooster said to the goat.

"Maaaybe you could use almond milk instead."

"Didn't know you could even milk an almond." Rooster said. "Almonds have teats? How's that done?"

"Get down here Rooster," Honus said. "We have a chance of getting to the castle today if we can stay on task."

Gertrude shrugged her shoulders. "I don't know; maybe fairies do it with their small hands?"

"Seems reasonable." Rooster agreed.

"Let's leave them both up there." Marren suggested.

"Let's go!" Honus called up at the pair.

Rooster spread his wings. "Like the mighty eagle, I soar!" He leapt away from the peak of the roof, gliding to the ground in a wide figure-eight. When he got there, he strutted back and forth. "Oh, that was soaring all right. Right there out on the wide-open sky. Soaring. You all looked like peasants from up there."

"I think the term is 'ants'", Marren said.

"Whatever. Something small and insignificant." Rooster flapped his winds. "In any case, completely unlike the majestic rooster."

The goat sat back on her butt as she judged the distance to the ground. "Here goes nothing." She bounced up and down until she started to slide down the roof. When she reached the end of it, she stuck out all four legs, hoping to land softly.

She landed on Rooster who was still strutting back and forth.

Not very softly.

"Hey how, I've got hollow bones you know!" Rooster pushed himself from under the goat. "All majestic birds have them."

"Sorry about that," Gertrude said. She looked up at Honus. "Hello there, young maaaan. I'm Gertie." She gave a curt nod.

"Nice to meet you." Honus nodded back. "I'm Honus. That's Marren."

Marren put his hands on his hips. "And now that the crisis is resolved, it was nice meeting you, goat." He tilted his head toward the path. "Let's get moving, daylight's wasting."

"I figured she'd come with us." Honus said. "I mean..."

"Why? It's bad enough we got this chicken..."

"Rooster. Majestic Rooster," Rooster corrected.

"... along for the ride," Marren ignored Rooster as he continued, "and honestly, I'm not sure why." He looked down at Rooster. "Well?"

"I'm trying to get home, of course." Rooster replied. "Then I'll definitely, positively, really most assuredly go my own way."

"Well, I appreciate the string of adverbs, Rooster." Marren said. "And since you're from here, there's no reason for you to come along." He said to the goat.

"She's familiar with the witch's castle," Honus offered.

Marren rolled his eyes. "You seen one castle, you've seen them all; big moat, towers, winged monkeys hopping around."

The goat nodded. "Well, that does describe her castle pretty well. But I've got a score to settle with that witch."

"Vengeance, huh?" Marren said.

"Exactly; there's no altruistic 'get more thoughtful or wise' for me." Gertie spat.

"That's gross." Marren said.

"It's something goats do," Gertie explained.

"I see. Well, we're going there to get a magical talisman from her so these two can get home," Marren said. "Not settle scores."

"Eliminating the witch was an option, if I remember correctly," Rooster tossed in. "I'm all for it."

"That is true." Marren nodded at Rooster. "But still. All we need to do is get that talisman..."

"You mean the magical silver star she wears around her neck except for when she takes it off to bathe?" Gertie asked.

Marren stared at Gertie for a long moment. "Fine. But only to the castle to get the star, then we go our separate ways."

"Deal." Gertie said. She started toward the path. "What's a Munchkin doing as part of this fellowship?"

"The Mayor asked me if I'd go along to help. He doesn't want the talisman falling into the wrong hands." Marren fell in step with the goat.

"But the Mayor's..."

"Just a moment." Marren turned and ran back into the cottage.

"Was it something I said?" The goat asked.

"Maybe he had to pee." Rooster offered.

"He wouldn't go inside to do that," Honus said with a head shake.

Marren came running out of the cottage- he held up the axe handle. "Better than nothing."

"I suppose so," Honus said.

Marren jogged up beside the goat. "Okay then, let's go." He looked at her. "You were saying?"

"The talisman falling into the wrong hands is bad but the Mayor's hands is okay?" Gertie said.

"It's better than the Blue Witch. Or any witch," Marren lied. "Can't let her get her hands on such a powerful talisman; it would really pitch the balance of power around here." He heaped on top of the lie.

"Well, as long as the other two witches are around, they can keep the Blue Witch in check.

"That's true," Marren said with a smirk. His aspirations included the deaths of the Witches of the East, North and South, then a nice cozy bed to share with the Witch of the West. Rumors were that she liked short men. Marren wanted to be that man. Hopefully by being the man that brought her the talisman of the Witch of the South.

"Seems pretty complicated with all these witches and wizards here," Honus said.

"It's typical local politics," Marren said. "You've probably got the same thing going on at home but you just don't notice it."

"I'd notice," Rooster said. "Thanks to my superior intellect."

Honus moved beside Gertie. "When was the last time you were in the castle?"

"Just a couple of days ago. I was running from the wolves after that witch kicked me out. I've been running for two days when I ended up on top of that little cottage."

"What can you tell us about it?" Rooster asked. "Some solid intel would come in handy."

"It's a formidable castle."

"That's good to hear," Honus said. "Right Marren? Wait, what was it?"

"That's helpful?" Rooster ruffled his feathers. "How is that helpful?"

"So how do we get in?" Marren said, ignoring Rooster. "What does she have as far as security?"

Gertie thought for a moment. "Well, she has a few flying monkeys on loan from the Witch of the West. Just to pass messages back and forth. Some flying squirrels as spies, and a furry four-legged thing with massive horns and wings that I've never seen before. And gorilla guards." She shuddered. "Big hairy beasts that'll eat anything that's put in front of them. Cooked or not."

"I'm at a loss for a joke about gorilla guards, but rest assured as soon as one pops into my head, I'll toss it out there." Rooster said. He flapped his wings several times and moved to Gertie's back. "Ahh, that's better. I'll keep a look out from here."

"So," Marren said. "Anything else?"

"No, not really; it's pretty secluded so they tend to see folks coming." Gertie thought for a moment. "Now that I think about it, the castle gate locks but I think the couple of dozen gorillas are the bigger deterrent."

Rooster sat and closed his eyes. "Gorilla guards...Gorilla guards." He mumbled. "Damn. Nothing's coming to mind."

"How can we get past gorillas?" Honus said. "I saw one in a traveling show once. It was a really big thing covered in black hair. And that one was alone."

"These carry pikes."

"What's a pike?" Honus asked.

Rooster started snoring.

"It's a long pole with a sharp metal end on it." Marren said.

"So how do we get past them?" Honus thought back to the traveling show. He had paid a nickel to go see the animals- a gorilla, giraffe, and a llama. Of the three, the massive silver backed ape impressed him the most.

"If we are able to get to the upper floors of the castle, we can avoid them completely," Gertie said. "They aren't allowed above the second level because the Witch of the South doesn't like their shedding."

"How do we get to the upper levels?" Honus asked. "It's not like we can fly up there."

"If you get a rope up to a second-floor window, you can just climb in. Then you can pull the rest of us up." Gertie said. "Easy peasy."

Honus glanced at the sleeping Rooster. "Oh no."

"There'll be no living with him if he's the key to the plan working," Marren said. "We really need another option." He frowned. "If only I had my pipe wrench still." He hefted the axe handle. "This is nice and all, but it's just not the same." He frowned. "And if the guys in the shop saw me with it, there'd be teasing for weeks. I need me a pipe wrench."

"Would that help you fly up there?" Gertie said.

Marren shook his head. "No, but it would let me wallop some of those gorillas on the head better'n this piece of hickory."

"Well, that might not be..." Began Honus. He stopped talking as he stopped walking. "This is just stupid."

The Red Brick Road forked in front of them.

"What's wrong now?" Marren asked as he too stopped walking.

Honus gestured. "The road forks. *Again*."

"What, where?"

Honus looked at Marren. "Right there! Just look at it!"

"He always get so excited at forks in the roads?" Gertie asked. "What's he going to do when we get to the bridge?"

Marren laughed. "No, that's not it. Apparently where he comes from, roads have signs that say what road goes where."

"No." Gertie said flatly.

"It's true. He explained it to me yesterday at the other fork in the Red Brick Road."

"You mean where one goes to the Kalidah stomping grounds and the other to the s'Mores killing fields?"

"See? Everyone knows where the road goes." Marren said.

"But what about folks that are visiting from other places?" Honus asked.

Marren started down the left Red Brick Road. "Don't be absurd. If you don't know where you're going, you shouldn't go there."

"No, but..."

"Right." Gertie added. "If you didn't know where you were going, when you got there, you wouldn't know you had even gotten there so why even bother leaving in the first place?"

"What?"

"The nerve of some people." Marren said.

"That's not what I'm..."

"Rude is what that is." Gertie added.

Honus just shook his head. "Never mind."

"Fine then." Marren gestured down the road. "Shall we?"

Rooster startled awake. "You great apes are only great at shedding!" He tilted his head to the side as he considered it. "No, no. Forget I even said that." He closed his eyes again. "Damn."

"So is there anything dangerous along this..."

Marren reached over and shoved Honus with the end of the axe handle. "I really need my pipe wrench."

"What was that for?" Honus asked as he recovered from his stumble.

"I can't believe you!"

"What?"

"You were, weren't you?" Marren snapped. "You were!"

"I were... was what?" Honus snapped back.

Marren looked at Gertie. "He was going to, wasn't he!"

"I heard him," Gertie said. "Seems pretty inconsiderate if you ask me."

Honus opened his mouth then closed it.

"What do you expect to happen when you ask a thing like that?"

"I don't see how just asking a question is going to cause something to happen."

"I say we wake up the Rooster and see what *he* thinks." Marren narrowed his eyes at the boy. "Want to see what *he* thinks?"

"You can if you want to." Honus chuckled. "You've been reading too much pulp fiction. It's not like asking if there is anything dangerous along the road is actually going to make something dangerous appear."

Marren stopped.

So did Gertie.

Both looked around nervously.

"See? What did I..."

A peal of thunder ran through the area as a funnel of billowing green smoke poured out of the ground and rose quickly.

Marren shoved Honus again.

"Damn it all, I'm trying to sleep here." Rooster opened his eyes and looked around. "What is going on?" He looked at the Witch of the West as she stepped out of a cloud of dark green smoke. "How'd she... What'd I miss? Some exposition would be nice."

"What?" Honus asked. "Expo what?"

"A nice flashback perhaps." Rooster suggested.

"Or a cut scene." Gertie said.

"A what?" Honus asked.

~~~~~~~~~~~~~~~~~~~~~~~~~

The Witch of the West leaned over her large black cauldron, careful to avoid the silvery tendrils of smoke coming from it.

"Once again then." She said with a sigh.

She gently lowered a long, hammered brass spoon into the boiling brown liquid. It was now far too powerful for mere wooden implements.

When the spoon touched the bottom, she moved it in slow, deliberate counter-clockwise circles.

Magia Balailo

Potenculo!

She incanted.

A dark green color crept up the tendril until the smoke was rising like green tentacles.

The witch leaned back, still keeping a hand on the spoon. "Nice." She remarked. "Finally, a good sign."

She leaned forward again and began to stir clockwise.

Colors green then; not silver
Yet still stores magic like arrows in a quiver

Imbued straw and wood
with magic to be used by me
As I say it should

She finished her incantation then gently pulled the spoon out. The bright brass spoon was blackened and pitted. "Bill!" she snapped.

A stooped money with cropped wings hopped into the room. "Ook?"

"Where is my broom?"

"Ook." Bell pointed matter-of-factly.

"Well *fetch it*, you oaf." She lifted the spoon over her head. "I'd brain you but you have none to hit."

"Ook, oook!" Bill started to point, then shrugged and hopped off.

"Make it quick, you lout!" The witch winced- her hand felt like it was on fire. She looked up to see the green fluid had run down the handle to her hand. With a flinch, she dropped the spoon but the damage was done- the green color began to spread down her arm. "No! No, no, no!" She held her hand out at arm's length as the color seeped down her arm. She grasped her forearm and concentrated on the magic as it seeped into her.

The color continued up her arm and through her body.

"Ook!" Exclaimed Bill. He held the broom at his considerable arm's length. Truth be told, the Witch of the West already had a definite green tinge to her and it was definitely not contagious as he had walked holding the witch's hand on many occasions since she had stolen him and clipped his wings. This new development made him reconsider.

The deeper green color crept up her neck.

"Akk?"

The Witch of the West snatched her broom from Bill "I'm fine."

"Ook?"

"Yes; it's... it's probably temporary. Once the magic leeches out." She took the broom and carefully lowered it into the caldron, bristles first. "Now to see if I got it right this time."

"Ook!" Bill hopped up and down. "Ooook!"

"What?" The Witch kept her eye on her broom- she had lost three so far. "I'm still busy here, Bill."

Bill shuffled to the far side of the room where a large crystal ball sat on an ornate iron pedestal. "Eeek!" He slapped his hands on the stone floor for emphasis. "Eeek ook!"

The Witch wheeled on the monkey. "What is it!"

Bill pointed at the swirling colors in the ball. He pointed at the sky then back at the swirling colors. "Oooh!" he added an interjection he used sparingly for emphasis.

"Now? After all this time?" She leaned the handle of the broom against the inside of the cauldron then quickly moved to the crystal and peered into it. In the swirling colors, she saw a boy and a rooster. They were on a red road. "Who?" She looked back at her broom. It seemed to be absorbing the magic without damage.

Bill slapped his hands on the floor again.

"I'll go see what these interlopers are doing, you keep an eye on my broom."

Bill patted his face. "Ook?"

"Just don't get any of it on you." She smiled. "I can't imagine the green would go well with your blue fur." She patted Bill on the head. "Keep an eye on things while I'm out."

Bill nodded at her. "Ook." He took several steps back toward the caldron- to get out of the blast zone.

The Witch raised her hands up high.

Flugas sur la Venton

Vamos!

She intoned.

In a cloud of deep green (more green that previously) smoke, she disappeared.

Bill looked at the broom. It burst into flames. "Ook akk," Bill cursed. With a sigh, he loped out, going to retrieve another broom. He hoped that as with other magical endeavors, the fifth time would be the charm.

~~~~~~~~~~~~~~~~~~~~~~~~~

"Well, that helps some," Rooster said. "Thanks for that."

"Quit shoving me," Honus said. "I don't see how any of this is my fault."

"Just be quiet from now on," Marren said. "We've enough troubles without you encouraging..."

"Uhm, boys..." Gertie said as she craned her head to look upward.

Everyone looked to where she was looking.

"Well, well; what do we have here?" The Witch of the West said. She cackled. "I always wondered if any others would show up."

"Show up?" Honus said. "Other what?"

"Helping him along, are you?" She put her hands on her hips and glowered at Marren. There was a twinkle I her eye. "*Munch-kin.*"

"Who me? I..." Marren stammered. "I'm just passing through. Minding my own business even. We just happened to cross paths just now. Well… so long, folks." Without another word, he scurried into the underbrush.

"That's true," Gertie added. "We only just met, this person whom I don't know and I." She looked to where Marren had disappeared under some bright yellow bushes. "Huh."

"Carrying a Rooster, I see." Now the Witch glowered at Gertie.

"What rooster? That Madame, is a birthmark," Gertie said testily. "And I'd appreciate you not mentioning it again. I'm very sensitive about it."

The Witch turned her attention to Honus. "And what is it you are doing here?"

"I'm not really sure," Honus said honestly.

"He's the straight man," Rooster offered.

"Well, I'm not one to judge, I'm sure," the Witch remarked. She eyed the young man, judgingly.

"See?" Rooster said. "You don't get that sort of material from a rooster or goat."

"So, we'll be on our way then," Gertie suggested.

"Don't I know you from somewhere?"

Gertie shook her head at the witch. "I won't say that you do."

"Can't" offered Rooster.

"I can't say that you do." Gertie said without missing a beat.

"I'm sure we've met somewhere. You look familiar."

"We Capras all look alike, so I've been told."

"That's racist." Rooster pointed out.

The Witch examined Gertie closely. "You cook?"

"Nope. Not I." Gertie looked down the path. "I graze." She opened her mouth. "Flat teeth, you see."

"That settles it then, I think." Rooster said. "Get back to whatever it is you do when you're not out and about, witch. Cooking. Canning. Polishing the stove. Making your man a sandwich, perhaps."

"What?" The Witch's eyes got large. "Keep it up and I'll stuff a turkey with you!"

Rooster staggered back several steps, then caught himself. "Oh, you think so, lady?" He strutted forward. "You're making powerful enemies. Powerful enemies!"

"Ma'am, we're going to be on our way now," Honus said, hoping to prevent any altercation. "Let's go, Rooster." He pointed down the path. "Let's go." He started down the path, Gertie falling in step beside him.

"Did I mention you were making powerful enemies?" Rooster cocked his head to the side to look at the Witch with one eye. "Did I?"

The Witch rolled her eyes. "Gads. And I was worried about you three buffoons. Whatever you're doing won't work and I've got better things to do." She clapped her hands over her head. A peal of thunder rolled through the area and in a cloud of greenish smoke, she disappeared.

"Yeah! Run away while you can!" Rooster strutted back and forth, scratching at the ground as he did. "Before I stuff a..." He looked around. "Stuff a.... a house with you!"

"Rooster! Come on!" Honus called from down the path.

With another scrape of the path, Rooster half ran, half flew back to Gertie's back. "I told her a thing or two." He said.

"You sure did," Honus said. "Scared her off, I imagine." He turned and looked up the path so Rooster couldn't see his smile.

"You see that?" Rooster asked Gertie.

"Yes. Very impressive." Gertie lied.

"Hah." Rooster squatted down on Gertie and closed his eyes. "She doesn't know who she's messing with." He said before falling asleep.

"She gone?" Marren asked as he stepped out of the underbrush.

"A lot of help you were, Marren." Honus said.

"Have you dealt with witches before?" He asked. "That Witch in particular?"

Honus shook his head at Marren. "No."

"Well she runs over the folks in my town... my *county* even, like an Oliphant over ants." He pointed toward where the Witch had been standing. "There's no way I'm going to do anything that makes her think she should come to my town and squash a bunch of us... me particularly, because she's annoyed." He put his hands in his pockets. "Remember, Honus; you're just passing through. I've got to *live* here."

Honus considered that. "That makes sense. I'm sorry. I'll try to make sure that I don't cause any extra trouble for you." He smiled. "I appreciate what you've done so far. I'm just glad the excitement is over..."

Marren rushed over and shoved Honus. "Stop it!"

"Come on!" Gertie exclaimed.

"He does it again," Marren said, "You just pile him over, Gertie."

Gertie lowered her head. "Sure thing. Heels over head."

"I think the phrase is..."

"Ahh!" Marren held up a finger. "No." He swiveled his finger around and pointed down the path. "That way for the rest of the day without another word. There's a trapper's shack at the edge of the Witch of the South's territory. We can stop there if we need to."

"How about just casual conversation?" Honus asked.

"Only really casual, uncontentious subjects." Gertie said. "I suggest sticking with politics and religion."

"I don't see how those two..."

"Ahh!" Marren held up the finger again. He waggled it back and forth then held it in front of his lips.

"Okay, okay." Honus said. "Hey, what about baseball? Can we talk about that?"

"Never heard of it."

Honus beamed. "I'll explain the game to you. You'll love it! Okay?"

"Fine." Marren said, unconvinced.

TWELVE HOURS LATER

"So, if the pitcher starts to pitch the ball then changes his mind, the people on the bases get to advance one base?" Gertie said.

"Yes." Honus answered.

"Sounds pretty unreasonable." Gertie said. "He should be able to change his mind."

A flying squirrel zipped by.

"Sounds like it stops some chicanery to me. Only rule I agree with," added Marren. "Overall though, there are too many rules in that game. No wonder it hasn't caught on."

"What do you mean?" Honus said. "It's real popular! It's the sport of royalty!"

"That's backgammon." Gertie said.

"Back what? Never heard of it," Honus said.

"I thought cricket was the game of royalty," Rooster offered.

"That's bait for fishing," Honus said with a smirk.

"What?" Rooster did a double-take at Honus. "Did you just..."

"Well, I've never heard of baseball." Marren said. "And we Munchkins are natural athletes."

"Obviously," Gertie said. "Told you we should have stuck to religion and politics. Never any disagreement with them two subjects."

"That has been my experience as well," Rooster added.

"I don't see how that's even possible." Honus said.

"Said the person who needs signs to know where he's going," Rooster cocked his head at Honus. "I'm not too sure we can take you seriously after that."

"Finally." Marren pointed. "The shack."

Just ahead on the path was a ramshackle shack.

"A trapper lives here?" Honus asked. "It looks like it's going to fall over."

"He doesn't live there now, of course," Marren said.

"Then why's it called the trapper's shack and not the abandoned shack or something else?"

"Don't be absurd." Marren pointed behind Honus. "The abandoned shack is over that way about an hour's walk."

"Right, and the woodcutter's shack is just past that." Gertie added. "Everyone knows that."

"Forget I asked." Honus said. He approached the shack and tried peeking in its only window. The dirt encrusted on it made it impossible to see inside. "Are we at the edge of that other witch's territory? Think she knows we're coming?"

Marren shoved Honus. "I'm telling you, when I get my hands on a pipe wrench, I'm going to break you of that annoying habit."

"Be reasonable." Honus said.

"I vow to poop in your mouth while you sleep," Rooster said. "And, in case you didn't know, we Majestic Wild Gallinus, like other birds, are..." He cocked his head to the side. "Soupy excreters."

Marren stuck out his tongue. "That is the truth."

A different flying squirrel zipped by.

"Fine, fine." Honus said. He pulled open the door to the shack. It came loose in his hand. "Great." He staggered back, dragging the door with him. "Just great." He moved to the side of the opening and propped the door there. "This thing is going to fall over on us if the wind picks up."

"We'll be fine," Rooster said.

"It's going to be dark soon and we definitely don't want to be out and about in the haunted forest then."

"Haunted? Come on, Marren." Honus looked around. "What if I don't believe in spooks?"

"Just because *you* don't believe in them doesn't mean *they* don't believe in you," said Marren. He looked around as well. "Believe me."

"Drat." Gertie commented. She looked into the shack. It was pitch dark inside. "Anyone bring a candle?"

"Candle or no, we shouldn't sleep in the outdoors." Marren said.

"I agree." Agreed Gertie. "I try to avoid the great outdoors whenever possible."

"But you're a goat," Honus said.

"So? What's that got to do with anything?" Gertie looked into the shack again. "It's awful dark in there though."

Honus shook his head at Gertie. "Come on; it's just an old abandoned old shack. What could happen in there? It's not like there's anyone lurking around in that thing. Come on." Honus gestured as he stepped in.

Gertie and Marren followed close behind.

"Wait. What did you just say?" Rooster asked as he too followed because he was still riding on Gertie and had been watching a squirrel on a nearby tree.

The fight was short.

And completely one sided.

"And that folks, is why I don't like that kid." Rooster said as he hung upside down from a pole.

"Listen..." Honus started. He was also upside down with his hands and feet tied to a pole.

"Not. Another. Word." Rooster threatened as he swung around at the end of a length of rope. Both of his feet were tied together and he swayed back and forth as the Goblin holding the pole over his shoulder shuffled along.

"Marren?" Honus said. "I just want..."

"I'm warnin' ya, kid." The Goblin holding Rooster said. "Keep quiet."

"You tell him, Gob." Rooster said.

"I tole you to stop callin' me that." The Goblin said. He jostled the pole making Rooster bounce against it. "Gonna roast ya."

"He didn't mean anything by it, noble Goblin," Marren said, hoping to build some inroads with their captors. "Remember his brain is the size of an acorn. Not huge as a melon like yours."

"Hey now!"

The Goblin chuckled. "A bite sized seso, huh?"

"I suppose so." Marren looked up at Rooster and gave a long wink. "Riiiight?"

Rooster nodded. "Oh right, right. An acorn. But remember that from a meek acorn, the mighty oak grows."

"That's poetical," the Goblin said.

"Want a poem about Goblins?" Rooster tilted his head to the side.

"Not particu'larly."

"Don't pester them," Gertie said. She was also tied to a pole that was being carried between two Goblins. "We've enough trouble at the moment."

"There once was a Goblin from Lower Ruttlocks..." Rooster began.

"Please don't." Marren said. He knew the tawdry poems that came from the Ruttlocks region. Upper and lower.

"Gots a cousin lives there," remarked the Goblin. "Wonder if it's her."

"Who was famous for her unusually large..."

"Rooster!" Gertie said. "Be quiet!"

"Personality?" The Goblin tried.

"That's it entirely," Marren interjected. "A pleasant gal, she was. Great personality."

"Yeah, it was so big, she'd buff it." Rooster said, skipping to the end of the limerick.

"I still don't see how this is my fault." Honus said. "I mean, there is no way that just saying 'I wonder if this will be a quiet trip' could..."

The Goblin carrying the front end of Honus' pole dropped it. He drew a dagger.

"See?" Rooster said. "Even a complete moron like Gob gets it."

The Goblin looked around warily for almost a minute. The other Goblins stood rock still. Finally, Gob sheathed his dagger. "Huh," he said as he picked up the pole. "Guess not."

"Told you," Honus said.

The Goblin carrying the front end of Honus' pole dropped it again. He put both hands on the arrow sticking out of his chest. "Gah." He said as he fell backwards.

The Goblin holding the back end of Honus' pole dropped it. He couldn't grab the arrow stuck in him because it was in his back. He fell over as well. Dutifully dead.

The two Goblins carrying Gertie dropped her to the ground and hid behind her. "Ambush!" One said.

"Who dun it?" asked the other.

The two carrying Marren dropped the Munchkin and immediately ran away.

"You want to put me down too?" Rooster asked. "So you don't end up dropping me. Hey, stop that!"

Rooster banged against the pole as the Goblin swung the pole around like a spear, searching for their attackers.

"I'm going to get sick!" Rooster said as he spun around on the end of the rope. "Put me down!"

The Goblin dropped the pole Rooster was tied to.

"That's better, thanks." Rooster said.

The Goblin didn't answer.

He was too busy being dead because of the arrow sticking out of his neck.

The two Goblins hiding behind Gertie assessed the situation with their combined keen intellect and experience in battle.

Then they both ran off.

No one said anything for a long moment.

"Well that was weird." Honus said. He rolled over onto his back and looked around.

121

Several human-looking soldiers came into the small clearing. One slung a longbow over his shoulder. They all wore thick fur coats that reached almost to the knees as well as a tall round fur hat adorned with colorful pompoms. Two held menacing looking pikes. The rest seemed to rely on the jagged swords hanging from wide leather belts.

"Yer coming with us," said the one with the longbow.

The squirrel sitting atop his hat leaned out. "Squeak!" He added, very satisfied with himself.

Without another word, the soldiers picked up the poles and began to walk down a secondary path.

"I have to say, you walk a lot smoother than that Goblin did," Rooster remarked.

"Who are you people? What do you want?" Honus asked. He looked at Rooster. "Who are these people?"

"They're soldiers of the Queen of the South," Marren said.

"On the bright side, we're not going to get lost finding her castle." Rooster remarked. "Or have any trouble getting inside."

"How's that witch even know we're coming?" Honus asked.

"Probably black magic." Marren tried.

"Black magic?" Honus said unbelievingly. "Come on. You expect me to believe that?"

"Then maybe a flashback cut scene." Rooster suggested.

"A what?"

~~~~~~~~~~~~~~~~~~~~~~~~~~~~

The Witch of the South stood on one of the many balconies of her massive castle. As far as castles went in the land of Oz, it was by far the largest. It was also the brightest since it was built with gleaming blocks white marble. And chrome fixtures, which were this year's brushed nickel.

Adding to the dazzling brightness of it was the magically maintained snowy landscape which ran almost a mile in all directions. The Witch leaned over the balcony, watching a snowy whirlwind meander around a frozen field. She touched her crystal and leaned her head to the right, sending the whirlwind to fill in a low spot in the snow. "Nice." She said, satisfied. "Very nice." She added a long sigh just because she thought it fit in nicely with her mood.

It did.

The witch turned and started to walk to the end of the long balcony- this one was her own private balcony that wrapped around three sides of the castle. That way she could keep an eye on the other Cardinal Witches. When she reached the corner of North and East, she heard a commotion below her so she leaned out to see what was happening.

A scurry of squirrels (as they were called when traveling in a group) seemed to be having a heated argument on the balcony below.

"What is going on? I'm trying to enjoy my snow devils!"

The squirrels all looked up at the Witch. None of them moved afterward.

"Well?"

A chattering started up as they decided who would bring the news. After a quick game of nuts - branches - trees, the losing squirrel clambered up the side of the castle to her balcony.

"What?"

"Squeak Squeakum squeak," the squirrel - named Branford- said.

"A what was seen coming this way?"

Branford made a circle with his tiny claws. "Squeakum."

"Soap bubbles don't just fly around the countryside all by them..." A thought occurred to her. "Hell's cymbals," she said. (She wasn't a fan of bells) Where did you see it?"

The squirrel pointed over the edge. "Squeak." It muttered meekly.

"Come on! Here? What do I pay you squirrels for if you let things get right up to the castle before you notice them?" She slapped her hand on the (gleaming) marble railing. "I mean honestly!" She peeked over the edge at the balcony below. "Honestly!" She shouted. She looked left and right at the other balconies. They were empty. Apparently, news of the unseen interloper had made it to the apes. She decided she would punish them later on- after they had forgotten.

The castle had been built with a great number of balconies, all with different purposes. The Witch's private one was to spy on her sisters. Another, on the other side allowed her flying monkeys to enter directly to their area without tracking mud (at best) or shedding fur as they roamed the castle. Directly below the squirrel balcony was a large, rail-less balcony was for the lone flying moose she had created. It was more of a failed experiment than a viable means of transportation, or as in the case of the monkeys and squirrels, spies. It was however, useful in striking fear in the local villagers who were not accustomed to seeing a thirteen hundred-pound creatures flying about. Mainly because there was only one dragon in the vicinity and he opted to spend his five-thousand-year lifespan napping decades at a time.

The Witch frowned. Of the sisters in her particular Cardinal Coven, there was only one that sent messages -or traveled- by bubble. She was also, out of her three sister witches, her least favorite, running a distant sixth in popularity. Mainly because she was also the pushiest. "Great."

A large soap bubble floated up and stopped right front of the Witch of the South.

"What now?" She reflexively put her hand on her talisman. "What do you want?"

The bubble throbbed as a voice emanated from it: "Greetings fellow Cardinal Sister."

The Witch of the South rolled her eyes- while the enchanted bubble allowed speech, it did not show images. She stuck out her tongue. "Same to you, Sister." She reached out to touch the bubble. It floated out of reach, avoiding her finger. "What is it you want, Northie?"

"You know I don't like it when you call me that."

"I forgot; forgive me, dear sister of mine." The Witch of the South did a little jig. "What is it you need?"

"We... have a new arrival."

"What? I... I didn't even know you were seeing someone. Congratulations, I suppose?"

"No, you dolt; not *that* kind of arrival. Another of those interfering Kansasians. Kansasonians?"

"I'd go with Hillbillies."

"Hillbillies. Thanks," the bubble said.

The war between the Cardinal Witches had been simmering for almost a decade when the self-identifying Wizard of Oz showed up. The arrival of another potentially influential (no one had actually seen the Wizard preform any magical feats) figurehead made it necessary for the establishment of alliances. In no time at all, the Witch of the West and East decided they would band together. Leaving the Witch of the South without an ally. Since she was easily the strongest of the other three, she wasn't worried. Very much. She was a little put out when the Witch of the North maneuvered herself into the good standing of the Wizard of Oz. He was by no means worthwhile as a mate, and again- had not displayed any magical abilities. So, the fact that no one picked her for an alliance rubbed her the wrong way. Which was why she had created her talisman.

"Another Wizard?" The Witch of the South smiled. With another wizard in the mix, she now had the opportunity to gain an ally. Something that she was sorely short of. "You don't say." She smoothed out her pearly-white dress. Then she tugged it down slightly, revealing a little more of her cleavage. Something she was surely not short of. "How unexpected; another wizard."

"No, it's some kid. Not a bright one either."

"When you say 'kid' how old are you talking here? Is there a tender-aged toddler wandering around Oz?" The Witch wrung her hands.

"Seventeen, eighteen. I don't think much older than that."

The Witch of the South now gave her dress a hearty downward tug- it was on the verge of showing more than just snowy white breasts. "That is a tender age... of a different sort."

"I suppose. I just wanted to let you know in case you come across the young man. So you welcome him properly" The Witch of the North schemed.

"Is he wandering around my territories?" She glanced at Branford.

126

Branford held up his tiny claws and shrugged.

The Witch of the South fought the urge to just squash Branford on her gleaming railing and shook a fist at him instead.

"I couldn't say," the Witch of the North said because she didn't want to. "I was just trying to be neighborly to a fellow Coven member. Helpful even."

"I would do the same," The Witch of the South lied because given the chance, she would drive a pike right through her associate's head then go out for ice cream afterwards. "Of course."

"Of course. Well... I have matters that need attending to."

"Still watching the broom construction channel?" She snickered. Not very quietly.

"Yes... well. Maybe we can discuss that another time," the Witch of the North said noncommittally because the last thing she wanted to discuss with any other witch or wizard within a thousand miles was the fact that the Witch of the West's broom-enchanting endeavors worried her greatly.

"Take care, Sister," the Witch of the South said even though she really, really didn't mean it. At all.

"Oh, before I forget..."

"Yes?" The Witch of the South slapped her hands on the railing.

Branford did a little hop out of the way.

"Can I borrow your moose?"

"Borrow my moose?" The Witch was caught off guard by the unusual request. "What for?"

"To terrify those stupid Munchkins. Just for the fun of it. I figure it could do that for a good week."

"He's pretty tame you know. A real pushover, really. And a sucker for cabbage."

"He's the size of a half dozen of them put together. They won't get close enough to find out he's a pushover."

"I suppose. But I want him back unharmed. Not like that monkey that died unexpectedly after you re-loaned it to Westie instead of sending him directly back to me." She sighed. "Bill was my favorite monkey."

"I didn't know. I feel badly about the entire incident," The Witch of the North coupled two lies together. Just for the fun of it. "I'll keep an extra watch on the moose," she said, earning a hat-trick of lies. Her second of the day.

"Returned unharmed," the Witch of the South said.

"Returned unharmed," the other agreed without mentioning what exactly had to be returned unharmed.

"Fine then. I'll send him your way in the morning."

"Thank you, Sister." With that, the bubble popped.

"Hah! Who's that old·hag think she's dealing with?" The Witch of the South said. She turned and loomed over Branford. "Listen up, you incompetent rodent!"

A flying squirrel did another little hope then sat on his haunches. "Squeak squeekly?" It asked meekly.

"As you heard, there is an interloper in my lands."

"Squeak."

"Find him."

"Squeak squeakum Squeak?" The squirrel punched its tiny fist into its tiny palm. "Squeakery?"

"No. I want him brought in alive. Keep in touch with my Woolly Warriors. When you find him, have them bring him to me."

The Squirrel stood on its hind legs. "Squeaker squeak!" It rendered a snappy salute then leaned back until it fell backwards off the balcony.

The Witch of the South leaned over the edge to see the squirrel execute a barrel roll before sailing down to the squirrels' balcony- to relay the mission to the others.

"Excellent. We'll have to see if this young man actually possesses any of the talents that previous, most annoying interloper *claims* to have." She glanced down at her breasts. They seemed ready to spill out of her top without any warning at all. A pang inside her made her add: "And perhaps he may have some more vigorous... virile... talents as well."

~~~~~~~~~~~~~~~~~~~~~~~~~~

"Well then- Does that help?" Rooster asked.

"What? Did what help?"

Rooster sighed. "Never mind."

"Squeak?" The squirrel asked as it leaned over the side of the furry hat. It pointed at Gertie, Rooster, and Marren. "Squeakum?"

The Woolly Warrior with the longbow rolled his eyes up to look at the squirrel. "You said the Mistress said to bring them to her."

The squirrel pointed at Honus. "Squeak." Then he pointed at the others. "Squeakery!"

"Now just a minute there, Master Squirrel," Rooster said. "Let's not be hasty."

"What?" Marren said. "What's going on?"

"Hate to muck it up. You know how she can be," the Warrior said. "Gonna bring them all just in case. Follow the order or get tossed to the border," he said, quoting the Warrior Handbook that they had all signed. In blood. Their own."

"That squirrel wants us dead." Rooster said.

"Squeakery Squeaktacious."

"Really most sincerely dead, in fact." Rooster translated.

Marren struggled against his bindings. "Let me out of here!"

"Shut up, Munchkin," the Warrior said. "No one's getting killed."

"That's a relief." Marren said.

"At least until the Mistress say so."

"Squeak!" The squirrel pointed at Marren.

"Who's this Mistress?" Honus asked.

"The Witch of the South, of course," Gertie said. "Now don't pester the nice guards that have said they won't kill us."

"Squeak!"

"Until our executions," Rooster translated again.

"How is it you understand that squirrel?" Honus asked.

"Can't you speak with other humans?"

Honus considered that. "I know a little German and Swedish. And a few words of Sak and Fox. But that's it."

"Oh, well. If you can speak fox, then you should understand Squirrel. They're pretty similar," observed Rooster.

"Like Goat and Trout." Gertie offered.

"No, Fox and Sak are Indian tribes. They're not animals. And there are lots of languages I don't know. Lots."

"Pathetic." Rooster said. "And kind of sad."

"Goats and trout speak the same language?" Honus asked.

"We're practically related." Gertie said. "In fact, if you consider the fact that..."

"You know why you don't hear us talking?" The bow-carrying Woolly Warrior interrupted.

"No?" Honus said.

"I could make a guess," Gertie said.

"Because we don't want to hear each other's voices right now. And we *sure* don't want to hear yours!"

"That was going to be my guess."

"Squeak!" Added the squirrel. He shook his little fist for emphasis.

"Huh." Rooster said, having never been insulted by a squirrel before.

The group traveled in silence for almost twenty minutes with only the sounds of the forest around them. As the sun dipped behind the nearby towering mountains, darkness came almost immediately.

"Wow." Honus said- having grown in up Kansas, he had never experienced such a sudden nightfall.

"What?" Rooster asked.

"It just got dark really fast all of a sudden."

"It's Dark Magic, of course," Rooster explained. "Happens all the time around these mountains."

"I don't think..." Marren started

"There was no statute of limitations on my earlier 'shut up' request," the Woolly Warrior said.

"How about a statue of light-atations?" Rooster said.

"Squeak!" The squirrel said. Because there was no such thing.

"I was just trying to lighten the mood," Rooster said. "Since it had suddenly gotten...darker?"

"Nicely done," Marren said

Within another twenty feet, the temperature dropped fifty degrees and a cold wind whipped past the group. The ground around the group was covered with almost six inches of snow and more was piled up on the tree branches.

"What in the world?" Honus said. "It's freezing all of a sudden."

"Shut up!"

"How about a statute of temperatur-ations?" Gertie offered, wanting to get in at least one play on words.

"Squeakery Squeak!" Cursed the squirrel.

"Wow." Rooster said. "Kiss your mother with that mouth?"

132

"Squeeeak." Cursed the squirrel again, just because his mother would have wanted him to.

As they continued to walk, the path ahead of them became inclined. Honus craned his neck to look ahead. In the snow-filled darkness, a gleaming white castle loomed at the top of the winding path. "I completely don't think I'm in Kansas anymore." He said.

"In Toto?" Rooster offered.

"I suppose." Honus let his head go slack. He wasn't sure if he was ever going to see his home again. He thought back to his friends and where he lived. Oddly, it seemed to be only vague memories. He concentrated to try and focus on specific people and places but couldn't. "What is happening?" He closed his eyes and tried to focus in on his memories. And to keep from shivering from the biting cold.

After a long thirty minutes, the group stood in front of a large wooden door. The lead Wooly Warrior kicked it with a thick, fur covered boot. "Open up!" He shouted.

A small hatch opened half way up the twenty-foot-tall door. "Who goes there?"

"Troop Eight," the Wooly Warrior said. "In control and back from patrol." He jerked a thumb over his shoulder. "We got them trespassers."

"We weren't trespassing," explained Rooster. "We were coming for a visit."

"In that case, we offered a lift to the uninvited guests who snuck into our territories unannounced," The Wooly Warrior corrected.

"Squeak." The squirrel reminded.

The Wooly Warrior grunted. "We offered a lift to the *unwanted*, uninvited guests who snuck into our territories unannounced."

"If you're going to put it that way," Rooster said, "you might as well stick with trespassers."

The man stuck an arm out and pointed to the sign hanging beside the door. "Can't you read?"

Honus looked up at the sign. "Trespassers will be persecuted." He read.

"I think it's prosecuted." Marren said.

The man flipped the sign. On the other side it read "The prosecuted will be violated."

"I think the saying is 'violators will be prosecuted'." Marren tried again.

"Does that sign have a side that says "Visitors always welcome?" Rooster asked.

The man flipped the sign over. "Nope." Then over again. "Still nope." And a third time. "Only got the two sides, sorry, chum."

"Norman!" The Woolly Warrior kicked the door again. "It's freezing out here! Let us in already."

"Fine, fine." Norman smiled wide then pulled his head in and shut the hatch. Several locks could be heard opening. The door swung open smoothly on well-oiled hinges. "Take them to the throne room." He said as he pointed. "The Mistress is expecting them," he added ominously.

~~~~~~~~~~~~~~~~~~~~~~~~~

Marren looked around as best he could.

So did Honus.

Rooster was asleep.

"I have a bad feeling about this," Gertie said.

The group was still tied to their respective poles except instead of being held, they were propped between ornate chairs.

"I thought the Mistress was expecting us," Honus said. "Where is she?"

"It's called 'making the little people wait'." Gertie explained. "She does it all the time."

"I resent that," Marren said. He tried to pull his hands free from the ropes. Again, with no success.

"Oh, it's not just Munchkins; we're all little people when it comes to royalty."

"She's royalty? Like a queen?"

Gertie looked at Honus- thanks to her long neck she could do so easily. "She lives in a castle. That's not where peasants live. Have you ever seen a peasant living in a castle?"

"I've never seen castle except in pictures." Honus admitted.

"It's your lucky day." Marren said.

"So why is she making us wait?" Honus asked.

"That way she can show who's in charge," Marren said. "All the witches do it. Royalty too. We're getting a double dose of it."

"It's all to make a grand..."

"Well, well, well," The Witch of the South said as she barged in through a large pair of double doors on the far side of the room. "What have we here?" She moved gracefully to the middle of the room. It was clearly marked by the enormous white, silver, and crystal-encrusted throne sitting there. She looked around, completely ignoring the tied-up group, deciding where to sit. After stepping toward a regular looking dining chair, she shrugged and climbed the three steps to the throne. She picked up her skirts, turned on the silver filigreed platform on the front of the throne, and sat slowly. "Ahhh," she said. "That's nice." She tugged down on the waistline of her dress.

No one said anything for a long moment.

The Witch looked left and right, again ignoring the tied-up group, and spotted one of her Woolly Warriors- the one with the longbow. "Ahhh; you found our wayward guests. Nicely done..." She gestured with her hand at the man. She never admitted to knowing the names of any of her Woolly Warriors. She would name the squirrels and monkeys in a glance however.

"Terrance," Terrance said for what was probably the thousandth time since he started working at the castle five years ago.

"Terrance!" The Witch said. "Where did you find them, Terrance?" As a rule, she would use the name of the Woolly Warrior repeatedly during the same conversation. If for some reason, they had to leave her sight even for a moment, she would once again act like she didn't know them.

"By the Woodcutters Shack." Terrance said. Defiantly.

The Snow Witch stared at Terrance. She reached up and put her hand on her talisman. This was a dance the two had performed many, many times.

"By the Woodcutters Shack, Mistress of the Ice and Snow where the Midnight Sun and the Cold Winds Blow." He said, using her full (self-imposed) title that only the Woolly Warriors were required to use. She let the squirrels call her Theresa. Even though it wasn't her name. Mainly because the squirrels had lisps and therefore had trouble pronouncing the 'th'. She changed the name the monkeys had to call her frequently and without warning. Having them beat with bamboo sticks when they invariably got it wrong. Just for fun.

"Excellent, Terrance." Finally, the Witch looked down at the group as if noticing them for the first time. "My goodness! Why are they tied up, you naughty Terrance?"

Terrance knew no matter what he said, it would be wrong. So he drew his dagger and simply cut the captives' binds.

When Rooster hit the ground, he startled awake. "Hey now, what's the meaning of that?" He strutted back and forth as he flapped his wings. "Most unpopular, that was."

"I agree, rooster." The Witch said. "Terrance, how rude you didn't do that sooner. I have a good mind to have you brought to my chambers later so I can teach you some manners..."

Honus stood up and flexed his arms, sore from hanging from them. All in all, at six feet once inch, he was well above average in height with a mop of sandy-blond hair. Thanks to spending all his days outside, he was well tanned, which emphasized his blond hair and blue eyes. And, thanks to his frequent running and carrying of heavy loads of newspapers, he was also very fit.

"But that won't be necessary, Terrance," The Snow Queen added quickly. "Not. At. All."

Terrance sheathed his dagger, relieved. "Yes, Mistress of the Ice and Snow where the Midnight Sun and the Cold Winds Blow. Will there be anything else?"

"No, Terrance." The Snow Queen shoo'ed Terrance off as she kept her eyes on Honus. Hungrily.

Relieved, Terrance quickly walked off.

"Miss Snow Queen," Marren said. "As you well know, we in Nexus City have always been friendly and willing hosts when you have traveled to our fine city."

"Mmm.hmmm."

"And we would like to apologize for any inconvenience we have caused you," Marren added in what was hopefully a diplomatic tone.

"Mmmm hmmm." The Snow Queen said, eyes trained on Honus. She bent over to adjust a strap on her shoe. Which was just fine and didn't need adjusting.

Honus watched the Witch as she bent over to fix her shoe. As she leaned forward, her breasts bulged out like the pale balls of pizza dough he had seen at Mister Cacchiatori's shop, on Sullivan Street, across from the medical center. To his shock, one of them also gave a peak of what could have been a slice of pepperoni. "Wha...wow." He said before he could stop himself.

The Snow Witch smiled as she righted herself, satisfied with the effect of her move. "Well then," she said. "Who do we have here?"

"Rooster's the name," Rooster said. "Rooster T. Rooster." He strutted back and forth. "I'm *sure* you've heard of me."

"Mmm hmmm." The Witch said. She was still looking at Honus.

"That's a goat." Rooster said, gesturing with his wing. "A run of the mill, you've never met her before because she's not famous, goat. An until now unbeknownst to you, aforementioned goat. Capra Incognita, you could call her."

"Baaaa." Gertie said. She moved closer to Rooster. So she could kick him if he continued to try and convince the Witch they had never met.

138

"I am Marren of the Lollipop Guild," Marren offered. The Witch still hadn't looked at him.

"And you are?" The Witch of the South asked.

"Honus." Honus said. He didn't know what to do for royalty or witches so he gave a short bow. "Pleased to meet you, Miss Mistress of snow and ice and..." He glanced at Marren. "The sun at midnight."

Marren put his palm over his face.

"You can call me Southie," The Witch of the South said with a smile. She leaned forward and put her hands on her knees. "My fit, young man." She was pleased to notice he glanced down at her breasts again. "And how young, in general, are you?" She asked. Hopping for a high number to satisfy local ordinances concerning age of consent.

"I'll be nineteen this August."

"August?" The Queen of the South sat back in her throne. "When is that?" She asked, hoping for a low number just to make herself feel better because if it was low enough, she was just going to round the years up.

"Well," Honus said, unaware that other cultures -and lands- had different names for months, "in just about two months."

"Well now, that is quite excellent to hear. And what is it you do, Honus who is for all intents and purposes already nineteen and of legal age?"

"Do?" Honus looked at Marren for help.

"As a job or trade," Marren said out of the side of his mouth.

"Not much, if you ask me," Rooster said. "In fact, without me he'd be completely useless." He hopped onto the seat of one of the chairs. "And that's being kind about it."

139

"I..." Honus hesitated. "I am a famous baseball player."

"I see. An athlete, then?"

Honus nodded. He was uncomfortable lying in general and especially to someone who was a witch. And apparently a queen. "Uh huh."

"And what are you doing here?" She crossed her legs, revealing her calves as she leaned back in her throne. She arched her back just to see what sort of reaction she could get from Honus.

Honus' eyes first dropped to her exposed calf then moved up quickly to her breasts. They lingered there for a few seconds before meeting her eyes. When he saw that she was watching him, he blushed.

"Very nice." The Witch of the South said, deciding that she did not care at all about the (more or less) twelve years between them. Or maybe it was ten years. The Witch was also prepared to conduct some rounding with those numbers as well.

Honus stared at the Witch, unsure.

The Witch stared at Honus, pretty damn sure.

Rooster cocked his head to the side. "We're here on a visit, Southie. Just seeing what there is to see. Just me, the Munchkin, that kid, and of course this goat whom you have never met before today."

"Baaa." Said Gertie. She leaned in close to Rooster. "*Shut up.*" She whispered.

"Oh!" Honus said, remembering why they were there. He opened his mouth then he realized that he couldn't very well tell the Witch why they were actually there. He closed his mouth. "Hmmm." He said instead.

140

Marren stepped beside Honus and patted him on the shoulder. "Well said, Honus." He smiled at the Witch. Being a grown man, he had realized quickly what was happening. He was not pleased that it wasn't happening to him, however.
Nevertheless, he forged on: "We are just passing through, Witch of the South, and ran out of daylight. If we could impose on your hospitality for the evening, we would be much obliged." He raised an eyebrow. "A place to bed down for the night would be... satisfying." He added just for fun.

The Witch smiled at the Munchkin. "I am sure... that can be arranged." She clapped her hands once.

After a moment, a badger ambled into the room.

Gertie turned her head so the badger wouldn't get a good look at her- they had met at culinary school and come up through the cooking ranks together.

"What is your bidding?" The badger asked in as bored and uninterested tone he could manage. He never used any title for anyone. Anywhere. Being a master chef, he felt (rightfully so) that no one was his equal and as such, no one required to be addressed with a title. In fact, he tried not to address anyone at all, given the chance.

"We have guests for dinner. Four of them."

The badger barely even looked at the interlopers. "It's too late to change the menu, of course. But I suppose I can have additional settings placed for them. And perhaps add a soup because the quiche will not go as far. I've had a beet broth simmering for a week now. I suppose I can serve it two days early." The badger decided on his menu three days ahead of time and would not change it even if the castle were on fire. He shrugged. "Won't be the same though. The last two days make it." He crossed his arms. "And it'll clash on the pallet with the

141

quiche." He uncrossed his arms and put them on his hips. "Not that anyone here besides me would notice."

"Fine, fine, Badger," the Witch said. She knew better than to argue with him. Mostly because he was a master chef, but also because he was going to prepare her food where she could not see him do it. "Thank you for that."

Without so much as another word or a bow, the badger scurried out.

Gertie nudged Rooster. "Go after him." She whispered.

"Why? I can't cook." Rooster said.

"I can." She nudged him. "Do it."

Rooster stretched his neck out. "Hey there, Southie. If you'd like I can go give your badger a hand with the cooking. I'm pretty famous as a cook. Not like this goat who doesn't know a thing about it."

The Witch of the South looked over. If it weren't for the fact that she never ate meat, she would have ordered the annoying bird cooked. "What?"

"I shall endeavor to help your cook...err cook the meal that we are imposing on him."

Glad to have him gone, she waved him off. "Fine. Go then." *One down* she thought.

Rooster strutting toward the door.

Gertie cleared her throat.

Rooster kept strutting.

Gertie cleared her throat a little louder.

When he was halfway there he turned and looked back.

"Take me with you," Gertie hissed.

"What?" Rooster said.

Gertie gestured at the door with her foot.

Rooster winked. "Riiight." He turned and walked to the door.

Gertie gaped at him.

When Rooster reached the door the badger had gone though, he turned around. "So why...Oh you stupid goat, get over here!" He flapped his wings. "Come here, you!"

Gertie looked toward the Queen of the South, worried. She was engaged in a conversation with Marren and Honus. She quickly scampered to Rooster. "What are you doing?"

"The best way to be unobtrusive is to not try at all."

"What? That' can't be true."

"It sure is. I have found that if you look suspicious, people notice right away. If you're loud and obnoxious, folks do their best to try and ignore you hoping that you leave them alone."

"So you're always trying to not look suspicious?" Gertie said.

"No, of course... Hey!" Rooster flapped his wings. "I resent that."

Gertie nudged the door open. "Let's go find Badger to get the inside scoop on the Witch."

"Like a scoop of ice cream?" Rooster stepped through the door. "That kind of scoop?"

Gertie shook her head and pushed past Rooster. "You're absurd. Let's go." She trotted down the hallway.

Rooster turned and started to close the door. As he did, he looked over at Honus, Marren, and the Witch.

The two men nodded in unison.

"Nice that they're getting along. Real nice." Roster cocked his head to the side. "As long as the narrative fits what I'm seeing."

The Witch rubbed her talisman as she spoke to the two men, causing wisps of frost to float up to her mouth. As she spoke, the wisps of frost intertwined with her words and made their way to their ears, beguiling them.

"Hope it's not a Human's only conversation and I can get in on the general agreementation that's going on," Rooster said as he moved closer to hear what she was saying. He strutted and flapped his wings as he went to make sure he was ignored.

He was.

~~~~~~~~~~~~~~~~~~~~~~~~~

Gertie caught up with Badger just as he pushed through the swinging door to the kitchen. "Mik," she said, using his animal name.

Badger startled at the sound of his secret name and turned quickly. "Gertude!" He said as he recognized her. "What are you doing here?" He looked around suspiciously. "Weren't you kicked out?"

"I walked out on my own." Gertie said matter-of-factly. "It just so happens that I got fed up with the menu limitations." She shook her head. "Vegetables, vegetables, vegetables. The bigger question is what are *you* still doing here?"

Mik shrugged. "I've got some feelers out, mailed some resumes. Entered a couple of competitions. When something looks solid, I'll be walking out on my own too." He turned and gestured at the long preparation table. It had a large pile of corn, broccoli, and cucumbers on it. "Prepping for tomorrow's lunch. I've the starts of what will be a delicious vegetable pot pie."

"Nice. Sorry about mucking up your meal plan for this evening."

Mik waved a hand at her. "Not another word about it. It's my pleasure to cook for a fellow chef." He went to the pot and stirred the soup. "What are you doing here?" He said without looking back.

Knowing she could trust the badger with her life, she answered truthfully: "I am trying to help that young man get home by stealing the Witch's talisman and giving it to the Witch of the North."

Mik turned his head as he continued to stir. "Gads, couldn't you come up with some sort of lie to tell me?" He turned to look into the pot again. "Try again."

"We're on holiday and just passing through. Seeing the sights and traveling the roads."

Mik turned his head as he continued to stir. "Oh! That's nice to hear. Having a good time at it?"

Gertie nodded. "So far so good."

"That's good to..."

Rooster burst into the room. "Chic Chiri Chí!" He crowed.

"Veramente?" Mik said, since like most Master Chefs, he spoke Italian.

"How is that possible?" Gertie asked.

"I don't know," Rooster said, "but that Witch out there has those two males agreeing to get rid of us after dinner." He flapped his wings. "Those turncoats! After all I've done for them." He gestured at Mik. "You're on the way out too, it seems."

"What?" The Badger pulled the spoon out of the pot and laid it on the stove. "Why?"

"She didn't give a reason," Rooster said. "I think she's gone crazy or something."

"You packed?" Gertie asked.

"Practically," Mik answered. "Can you give me a hand getting my stuff together?" He started toward a door at the back of the kitchen.

Gertie nodded. "Watch the door, Rooster, we'll be right back."

Rooster saluted them. "Sure thing. I've got this covered. Go pack."

After the other two left, Rooster strutted back and forth. "Oh yes, I'm on guard duty." He sniffed. "Guarding the door." He sniffed again. "Guarding dutifully." He looked at the steaming pot. "That smells almost good." He sniffed again. "It's practically on the verge delicious." He walked over to the pot and peered in, smelling deeply. "Ahhh. So close."

Rooster looked around the kitchen- it seemed to be well apportioned with all manner of cookery spread out throughout it. Across the kitchen was a large hearth with a pot hanging in it. Strangely, there seemed to be red line painted on the floor separating the room in half. The line continued up the walls and even across the ceiling. "Odd," Rooster said as he strutted over to the line. "Most odd." With a little hop, he jumped the line to the 'other' side of the kitchen. As he did, the smell of meat cooking overtook him. The cold hearth that before seemed to have just an empty pot in it now was filled with red-hot coals. "Oh, that's nice as can be." He walked over to the fireplace where an entire pig was cooking on a spit. He looked back across the kitchen. "That's what's missing."

After searching for a moment, he found a knife and cut a large portion of meat off the thigh of the pig. "Just about right." He hopped back across the kitchen, holding the piece of meat in his raised claw. He crossed the red line and with several flaps, made it back onto the stove. "In you go, you delicious piece of meat." With that, he dropped it into the pot and stirred it. "Beets and bacon. Nothing's better." He turned and looked across the kitchen. Not only was the pig no longer visible, there wasn't even a hint of its aroma- just the empty hearth and the pot.

"Odd." Rooster said as the door opened at the back of the kitchen. Gertie and Mik came in, Gertie was pulling a wagon by a strap attached to the front of it.

"What's odd?" Mik said. Because Gertie's mouth was full.

"Generally, things that aren't normal."

Gertie let the tongue of the wagon drop. "Or things that aren't even."

Rooster cocked his head to the side. "You joining our merry band of misfits? Remember that I am in charge if you do join and you will be starting at the bottom of the pecking order. Gertie's just above you."

"Goats don't peck," Gertie pointed out.

"Neither do badgers."

"I'll be the one doing the pecking." Rooster said.

"I don't think that's what that phrase means, you loon."

Rooster stared at Mik. "That's one. Two, now that I consider the addition of 'loon'."

147

"Two what?"

"Pecks. Or peck, I should say. I have duly considered your remark and decided that the 'loon' was not an insult, comparing me to the majestic Loon." Rooster straightened out his neck. "A delightful bird. Bright plumage and honorable as the day is long."

Mik exhaled loudly. "It's a good thing I'll be going my own way then."

"I'll just keep a tab in case you ever do join our ranks. There is no expiration date on pecks, you..."

A bell hanging from a bent piece of metal by the main door of the kitchen jangled angrily as someone pulled the string attached to it.

"What's that?" Rooster asked.

"A bell, you booby." Gertie said with a smirk. "Blue footed boobie, in fact."

"Another noble member of the bird family. I appreciate the compliment." Rooster strutted back and forth. "Their dance goes like this." He stuck out a foot as he stopped, then he strutted the other direction for about three feet. When he got there, he stuck out the other foot, head tilted away from it. "If I do this a few more times, I'll get a date with one." He looked at the bell. It was still jingling. "If that racket would stop."

"Once the meal is served." Mik moved to the stove. He sniffed. "What is that smell?"

"Soup's on!" Rooster said. "And I'm starving. Where do we eat?"

"Back in the main room." Mik pointed at the door they all originally came in. "They've moved the table in by now. Chairs too."

The bell clanged even louder.

"Let's go then," Rooster said. "After you, Gertie." He nodded at Mik, "and you too, of course."

Mik shook his head. "I don't eat out there."

"Why not?" Rooster asked.

Gertie nodded. "It's annoying for a chef to eat with the folks they cook for, of course."

"What?"

"This is too hot." Mik said.

"Why's the Vichyssoice cold?" Gertie offered.

"Where's the salt?"

"This needs pepper."

"More cheese, please."

"Where's the ketchup?"

Mik gasped. "The K-word," he said in a whisper.

"Okay, okay," Rooster said. "I get it; cooks can't take constructive criticism."

"Cooks? Cooks? **COOKS?**" Mik looked from Rooster to Gertie and back again. He put his hands on his hips. "I'll have you know..."

An ape barged into the room. "Food ready?"

"Yes, Earl," Mik sighed. He gestured at the pot. "Food ready. Start with the soup. I'll whip up a salad to cleanse their dull palates before the main course."

"Not right." Earl said. "Eat soup in bowls, not palates." He rubbed his chin. "Think they called plates. You got accent or something?"

"That's what I'm dealing with." Mik gestured at the ape. "Every day."

"You poor dear," Gertie said.

"Let's go, Earl. My belly's ready for some food." Rooster said. "Before I waste away to nothing."

Earl stomped over and picked up the steaming pot of soup. "Smell good. Better than usual."

Mik's head drooped. "That hurts most of all."

"While we're young, Earl." Rooster started for the door. "And the soup's hot." He cocked his head. "It's hot, right?"

"Yes." Mik seethed. "The. Soup. Is. Hot."

"I'm so sorry," Gertie said. She turned to Rooster. "Get going, you barbarian." She lowered her head. "Before I bounce you all the way to the table."

Rooster scampered out of the room. "Hot soup, coming through!" He warned as he went, Earl close behind.

"Want me to wait here?" Gertie asked.

Mik shook his head. "I'll pick out my favorite utensils and add them to the wagon while you eat." He sighed. "After I whip up a nice Kaiser Saucey Salad to cleanse their palates."

"Wow, a Kaiser Saucey salad?" Gertie was impressed. "You've mastered it?"

"Oh yes; it leaves no trace on your palate at all. It's as if you never even ate any of the usual suspect foods that will tarnish a palate." Mik said. He gave a short bow. "You're welcome."

"I'll try to get them to appreciate it."

"Good luck with that." Mik pointed at the door. "You need to get going; if you're late, you will lose your spot at the table."

Gertie nodded, then because she was also hungry, trotted out of the kitchen. When she got back to the main hall, an ape was picking up her chair.

"Thanks for that," Gertie said as she practically galloped the last half dozen yards, then clambering up on the chair. "You are a gentleape, if there ever was one."

"Ook," the ape said, unconvinced of the compliment. Mainly because he didn't understand it. At all.

~~~~~~~~~~~~~~~~~~~~~~~~~

The Witch of the South picked up her napkin and snapped it loudly. "Well then, now that we are all here." She raised an eyebrow at Gertie. "We can begin." She looked at Earl. "With…"

"Food." Earl said. He held up the pot. "In here."

Gertie leaned forward. "It's beet soup."

"Food it is," the Witch said. She looked around the table. "Where's the salt?"

"But you haven't even tasted it yet!" Gertie exclaimed.

"Salt is here, my Queen," Honus droned. He reached forward. "All that you ask for, you receive." He lifted the salt bowl from the table and passed it slowly to Marren who was between him and the Witch."

"It might not even need salt." Gertie tried again. "If it did, I'm sure that…"

"Here is your desire," Marren said as he placed the salt in front of the Witch.

"You are both such helpful gentlemen, I must say," the Witch said.

"Always agree," Honus said as he nodded.

"What?" Gertie said. "What's gotten into you two?"

Earl moved beside the Witch and ladled soup into her bowl. "Soup's on." He continued around the table, putting soup not only in the bowls, but also on several parts of the tablecloth. When he finished, he gave a big smile. "Good?"

"Good what?" The Witch raised an eyebrow.

"Good, Miss..." The ape thought back to the last name he had used. It was several days ago because he had been off the past two. He remembered it started with an 'm' but that was it. "Miss Emmmm...mmmm"

The Witch smirked at Earl.

"Miss Marcie?"

The Witch smiled. "You know, that's not even close, but with recent events raising my spirits, I'll accept it." She shoo'ed him away. "Off with you, Earl."

Relieved, the ape scampered off, pot under his arm.

The Witch picked up her spoon and dipped it into the soup. "Well then."

"That's all the invitation I need," Rooster said. He dipped his head down and began slurping up the soup. He moved his beak around to grab a stray piece of pork. "Mmmm!" He said.

The Witch put her spoon down. "I... uhhh..." She looked at Marren. "He may need to go sooner rather than later."

"As you wish," Marren said.

Gertie dipped her spoon into her soup. "What has gotten into you, Marren?"

"Nothing, Gertrude," the Witch said. She dipped her spoon in her soup as she narrowed her eyes at Gertie.

Gertie dropped her spoon. "Wha...what? Who?"

Rooster picked up his head. Soup dribbled down his beak. "Gertrude? Errr... That's an odd name for a goat. I thought you were a Betty."

The Witch brought the spoon up to her lip.

"I... I am," Gertie lied. "You must have me confused with some other goat. Are you saying all goats look alike?"

"That's racist... and speciesist, I might add." Rooster said.

The Witch put her spoon back in her soup. "Are you saying you aren't Gertrude the Goat, the famous chef? I find that hard to believe."

"You do?" Rooster cocked his head to the side.

"Yes." The Witch hissed. She picked up her spoon again- the soup was getting cold from all the stirring. She once again dipped it into the soup and brought it up.

"I once knew this chick that laid chocolate eggs." Rooster said.

"What? That's absurd." The Witch said, caught off guard by the comment. She lowered her spoon but didn't put it down.

"Frogs are turtles that have lost their shells."

"Everyone knows that." The Witch said. She brought the spoon up again. "What are you getting at?"

"I'm just trying to establish a baseline of what you find believable or not. To keep the conversation moving along." He turned to Gertie. "Right, Betty?"

"Right." Gertie/Betty picked up her spoon. "Great soup."

Rooster nudged her with his foot.

"Needs salt?" Gertie tried.

"My thoughts exactly." Rooster said. "Now that we're on a new subject, pass that salt this way when you're done with it, Southie."

The Witch put her spoon back down with a sigh and handed the salt bowl to Marren. "Send this down there."

"As you wish," Marren monotoned. He stood and walked the bowl to Gertie/Betty.

The Witch picked up the spoon, dipped it into the soup and ate it before anyone could say anything else.

Rooster gave a nod to Marren. "Put a sixteenth of a spoon in my soup before you go, kid."

Marren put the salt bowl down beside Gertie and picked up the tiny spoon in it. It had a serrated edge to help sprinkle the salt. He scattered salt across Rooster's bowl. Almost a whole spoonful.

"Perfect, I'd say." Rooster said. Then he went back to slurping up the soup.

"Guh guh guh guh guh guh," said the Witch. She dropped her spoon, letting it splash in her soup.

"I'll do my own salt," Gertie/Betty said to Marren. "Back to your end of the table." She narrowed her eyes at him. "Where all the Humans are sitting."

"Buh buh buh buh buh." Said the Witch. She gawked down at her bowl.

"My sentiments exactly," Rooster said. "What do you think about all this weather going on around here, Southie?"

"Meeh meeh meeh meeh." The Witch said. Now her hands were up on her throat. "Tah," she added. She clawed at her throat.

"Pretty self-centered, aren't we." Rooster exhaled loudly. "How are *you* today, Southie?" Rooster looked at the Witch. She seemed slightly smaller than just a moment ago. "Are you slouching?"

"Mel mel mel mel mel!" The Witch said. She slapped her hands on the table. It was about chest high to her. "Ting!"

"What is going on?" Gertie asked. "Honus, help her! What's wrong with you?"

Honus -and Marren- continued to stare straight ahead.

"She's having a conniption, or something." Rooster said. "Maybe she needs the salt as well."

Realization washed over Gertie. "Wait; what did you do?" She picked up her spoon and tasted the soup. "Meat! There's meat in this soup!"

"Pork to be exact," Rooster said. "Goes great with beets." He shook his head. "Figured a famous chef like yourself would know that."

"Whaaata whatta whatta!" The Witch shrieked. The table was now even with her chin. "Whirl whirl whirl dah!"

"Think she needs the salt?" Rooster tasted his soup again. "Mine's a little too salty. A dash would have been better." He nodded at Marren. "You ruined my soup, you dolt."

155

"You idiot!" Gertie said as she hopped off her chair and trotted around to the head of the table.

Only the very top of the Witch's head was visible now. "Hay hay hay hay" She said as her head disappeared below the table. "Tah!"

"Well, that's a little harsh," Rooster said. He craned his neck to try and see her. "You hiding under the table Southie?"

Gertie skidded to a stop beside the Witch's chair as she oozed onto the floor. "Gads!" She looked over at Rooster. "She doesn't eat meat, you idiot!"

Rooster slurped some more of his soup. "She does now. She's a better person now because of it, too."

"She's not a person at all because of it!" Gertie looked down. "She's a puddle!"

Honus shuddered as if he were startled awake. "What happened?" He shook Marren. "Hey, what happened."

"What?" Marren looked around. "Where am I?"

"You're missing the first course is where you are," Rooster said. "And it's dee-licious, if I don't say so myself."

Marren looked at the bowl in front of him, then around the table. "Where's the Witch of the South?"

"No idea," Rooster said.

Gertie put her front legs on the table. "Rooster killed her!"

"Really?"

"Yes!"

"Wasn't that the plan all along?" Rooster looked at Gertie's bowl. "You going to finish that? That Munchkin went light on your salt."

"Rooster! You killed the Witch!"

Rooster hopped to Gertie's chair. "Okay, okay. You don't have to shout it." He looked towards the door the ape had gone out earlier. "No sense in raising the alarm." He cocked his head to the side, "until after dessert at least."

Honus looked under the table. "Ewww. What happened to her?"

"Rooster doctored her soup and it poisoned her."

Honus pushed his bowl away. "Poison?"

Rooster slurped some of Gertie's soup. "Poison? What do you take me for? Poison. I just added a little pork to it is all."

"Well, beets and pork do go together," Marren said as he pulled his bowl a little closer. He peered into it. "You sure its safe?"

Rooster slurped more soup. "I'm on my second bowl. Don't be a paper belly."

Not wanting to be a paper belly, Marren pulled the bowl closer and picked up his spoon. "Don't you go calling me names." He dipped it into the soup and sipped it. "Hmmm. Damn, that *is* good."

"Needs salt, doesn't it." Rooster said flatly.

"Maybe just a tad."

Rooster hopped onto the table and pushed the salt over to the Munchkin with his nose then returned to Gertie's chair.

"She's dead?"

"That Honus, my young man is the understatement of the chapter," Rooster said. "And they're pretty long if you don't count the tildas."

"What?"

"Never mind." Rooster returned to eating the soup.

Marren picked up the salt spoon and lightly scattered salt over his bowl as Mik entered the room. "What the hell!" Mik cursed. "I knew I should have stayed in the kitchen longer." He marched up to the table. "And what are you doing, *Munchkin*? What are you saying about my soup making abilities?"

Marren put the spoon back in the salt bowl. "I was uhm... It was..." He looked at Rooster for help. "Rooster?"

Rooster pointed at wing at Mik. "Your cooking killed the Witch of the South." He said flatly. "Dee Eee Aye Dee, dead."

"Huh." Mik said.

"Not surprised?"

"I'm surprised you can *spell*." Mik said.

"We're going to have it out, me and you," Rooster threatened. "Right after I deal with that youth at yon end of the table." He pointed at Honus.

"What? Me?" He looked down at the soup. "I didn't do anything."

"Not right now. But you did earlier. There is no statute of limitations on come uppances." Rooster said.

Rightfully so.

"The bigger issue is what are we going to do about the Witch." Gertie said.

"What's the issue with the Witch?" Mik looked around. "Where'd she go?"

Gertie gestured under the table.

"The witch issue seems to have become its own solution." Rooster said as Mik looked at the remains of the witch. He cocked his head to the side. "Nice, huh?"

"Not really." Marren stuck out his tongue. "Gross is what it is."

Gertie pointed at where the Witch of the South had been sitting. "This is going to be an issue. We are in the middle of her territory and the most likely suspects for her murder."

"Murder?" Rooster hopped onto the table. "Mur-der? That's a little heavy handed. And as someone who had nothing to do with it, inaccurate."

"What killed her?" Honus asked. "It was... sudden."

Marren looked at her bowl. "It was Rooster doctoring her soup, of course."

"I'd prefer to believe Mik poisoned her." Rooster hopped back onto the chair. "The culprit has been revealed." He pointed at Mik. "After years..."

"I've been here four months," Mik corrected.

"Months," Rooster continued, "months of tormetation and subjugation, this fine badger snapped." He slapped his wings together. "Oh yes, snapped! And offed the well-endowed witch."

"First off," Mik said. "Tormentation isn't a word and since I'm better than anyone in this dump, I'm the least subjugated one here." He pointed at the floor. "Go talk to those squirrels and apes if you want to talk subjugated. She torments... tormented then just for the fun of it. And that doesn't change the fact that..."

"I see." Rooster tapped his chin. "Very interesting, this new information." He pointed at Mik again. "So you had accomplices!"

Mik shook his head. "You're nuts. And you're responsible!" He pointed at the Witch's seat. "She doesn't eat meat. At all. Ever."

"Ever?"

"No. There's even a powerful spell to even keep the *smell* of meat cooking away from her meals."

"That red line, huh?"

Mik pointed a claw at Rooster. "That line *you* crossed, took some meat that the *apes* eat, and put it in *her* food!"

"Well, I..." Rooster stammered. "Let's not jump to..."

"I think we need to address this issue that could easily have us killed." Gertie said. "We're all prime suspects."

"That's true," Marren said. "Even if she was mean to her subjects, now that she's dead, they'll probably want to exact justice on us." He pointed at himself. "And I sure don't want to be lynched by some ape!"

"Well, we need to do something."

"I agree wholeheartedly. And I think the first thing we should do to address this tragedy is to cut that quiche into four equal slices instead of five." Rooster looked at Mik. "Unless you're having some."

"I had pork," Mik said. "*From the ape side of the kitchen.*" He peeked under the table. "Those cleaners aren't going to be pleased at all."

"We'll discuss that after we have that quiche." Rooster said. "This soup has aroused my appetite but not bedded it down. Even with the added pork. The quiche is the thing."

"How can you think of eating at a time like this?" Honus said.

"What, you mean at dinner time?" Rooster asked.

"Rooster!" Honus gestured under the table. "You *killed* her! She's dead! Don't you care?"

"Listen." Rooster hopped onto the table. "I understand you're upset." He spread his wings out. "We're all upset. Rightfully so." He held his wings out plaintively. "But correct me if I am wrong, the plan all along was to knock off the Witch and steal her medallion o' power. Am I right?"

Everyone looked someplace different in the room.

"Am I wrong or am I right?" Rooster said as he brought his wings down.

"You're right, I suppose." Marren said.

"Great." Rooster hopped back to his own chair. "Great. Here's what we're going to do." He pointed at Gertie. "You get back to your seat." He pointed at Honus. "You get that medallion." He pointed at Marren. "You eat your soup before it gets cold." He turned and pointed at Mik. "And you, good Sir, cut that quiche into four even pieces." He cocked his head to the side. "Cardinal pieces, if you'll allow the good-natured ribbing of the recently most sincerely dead Witch of the Cardinal Coven."

"I don't think I will."

"Okay then. Four even slices and be quick about it."

Honus stood up with the medallion. He was holding it with his napkin. "At some point someone's going to come in here and see what's happened." He said as he sat back down.

"What?" Rooster flapped his wings. "What did you just say? Marren, if you please." He gestured at him.

Marren reached up and slapped the back of Honus' head.

"Hey!" Honus complained. "What did I..."

"That's why we're still going to have it out." Rooster said. "Why would you even say..."

The door on the far side of the room opened. An ape lumbered in. "Hey Mistress..." He began.

Rooster gestured at Honus.

Marren slapped the back of Honus' head again.

"Hey!" Honus frowned.

"Uhm..." The ape said.

Gertie looked at the massive beast. "Sorry, what is it?"

The ape furrowed his hearty brow. "Now I don't remember."

"Was it about the Witch?" Rooster asked, helpfully.

Gertie tried to kick Rooster under the table but since he was standing on the seat, she missed. The table thumped and the glasses shook as she kicked the table.

"Yeah, that it." The ape smiled showing large white fangs. "Thanks! Where she..."

"She had to go make water." Rooster deadpanned.

Gertie turned to try and get a better angle at kicking Rooster.

"Wot?"

Rooster hopped onto the table. "Her back teeth were floating."

"Not sure if that proper way talk about a woman. Even if they mean-hearted Witch." The ape said uncomfortably. "Decorum is called."

"I mean, honestly; don't you have *any* manners?"

"I agree with Gertie," Marren said. He looked at the ape. "Sorry about him. Do you want us to pass a message to her?"

"Message to who?" The ape said.

"The Witch of the South, of course!" Rooster pointed at the far end of the table. "Miss Puddles."

The ape looked down, sheepishly. "I'm not comfortable with such terms in mixed company."

"Roosters and Humans," Rooster winked. "Understandable, my good ape." Rooster turned to the Simian. "What is it you need, Pongo?"

The ape looked around the room. "Who Pongo?"

"Aren't you?"

The ape unfurrowed then refurrowed his massive brow. "No." He answered. "That Orangutan name, of course."

Because it is.

"Take it easy; it was just a guess. You look like a Pongo is all." Rooster said. "What's the message?"

"Badger packed up his stuff. Looks like he going to make run for it. We'll keep eye out."

Mik turned to face away from the ape.

"That it?"

"We hold his last check for not giving notice."

"Damn," Mik said.

"Fine, fine. We'll keep an eye out as well, my good Simian."
Rooster said.

With a curt nod the ape turned and left.

"That was close." Gertie said.

"It sure was," Rooster agreed. "I was worried we'd have to skip
the second course there for a minute."

"I don't see how eating is a priority right now." Gertie
snapped.

"Know any good restaurants around here?" Rooster asked as
he turned to face Gertie.

"Uhm..."

"Hey, badger, know of any good places to eat around here?"
Rooster tuned to face Mik.

"There aren't any, actually. The closest tavern is about five
hours away."

"Which means walking through the night in a dark and spooky
forest just to have breakfast." Rooster held up a wing and took
a deep breath. "Or bedding down in the dark and spooky oh,
and cold forest all night long, walking all morning then finally
arriving at said tavern in time for a late lunch which they will
probably give us for free because they are kind-hearted folks
there and would have no trouble just giving way free meals to
the likes of us."

"At some point someone's going to notice the Witch of the
South, the owner of this castle, is gone." Honus said. "Then
we're pinched for sure."

"Only the meek get pinched," Rooster said. He pointed at Mik.
"Get to cutting that quiche, badger." He did a double-take at
Marren. "Eat that soup while it's hot!" He hopped onto the
table and strutted to the bell beside the Witch's chair.

"Don't!" Gertie said as she hopped off her chair.

Rooster picked up the bell in his beak and rang it furiously.

"Stop!" Mik said. "What are you doing?"

Rooster dropped the bell then flapped to the window, getting it open just as two apes came into the room. They lumbered to the edge of the table.

"Mistress?" The said in unison. They looked around the room confused.

"See you tomorrow then, Southie!" Rooster shouted out the open window. He waved furiously. "And good luck with that no-good sister of yours!" He did a double-take at the apes then looked back out the window. "What?" He craned his head out. "If you say so!" He shouted. Then he waved again. "Thanks!"

"Wots going on?" Said one of the apes.

The other frowned. "Most irregular." Because it was.

"Oh, hello there." Rooster flapped his way in front of the two apes. "Southie said she needed to deal with her sister of the West with some important matter of Coventry and that we were to stay the night and have a great breakfast before you give us a wagon and something dependable to pull it so we can continue our tour of the lands." He cocked his head. "Oh, and we need a mop."

"In the morning?" the ape asked.

"Err... The mop is for now," Rooster explained "The other stuff is tomorrow."

"Wot you got to mop?"

Rooster pointed at Marren. "The Munchkin spilled a drink." He elbowed the ape. "He was doing a song and dance routine. You know how those Munchkins can be."

The apes laughed.

"That true enough," one said.

"How'd you elbow him without elbows?" The other asked.

"Never you mind, my observant ape." Rooster said. He looked at Mik. "Do you think that perhaps the quiche will get served before the next set of tildes?"

"What's a tilde?" Honus asked.

"I'll explain it when you're older." Rooster said.

"I'll get it," Mik said, "If you think it's worth the risk of delaying."

"Well," Rooster raised his beak at the ceiling. "If you don't think you can make a quiche that's worth the risk, then maybe we should just wait to eat until tomorrow. Late tomorrow. No sense putting our palates in jeopardy with a mediocre meal. We'll just wait and go eat from a paid-by-the-hour tavern short order cook."

"What... what?" Mik fumed. "Are you saying my quiche isn't what it ought to be?"

"Serve it and we'll decide for ourselves." Rooster said.

"Fine then." Mik stormed out.

"You sure know how to make friends," Marren remarked.

"Tildes approaching." Rooster warned. He turned to face the apes. "If you two gentle apes would be so kind as to have someone send a mop this way so we can clean up our mess, that will be it for the night." He saluted them. "As you were."

"We was picking fleas off the squirrels," admitted one.

"Tasty and helpful," said the other.

"Gah. Okay then." Rooster shoo'ed them away. "Off with you both." He looked over his shoulder.

"What're you looking at?" Honus asked.

"Nothing." Rooster walked back to his seat. "See? This is why I'm in charge."

"I don't see what you've done," Gertie said. "Besides boss people around."

"That, my dear goat, is the sign of a good leader." Rooster flopped down in his seat. "We have a safe, warm place to stay, what should hopefully be a good second course on the way, and a means of travel to be given to us in the morning that will have us far away when they figure out what happened. *That's* the stuff of leadership."

"Before the tildes?" Honus asked."

Rooster looked over his shoulder. "Just before, in fact."

Mik entered the room, holding a large tray in his paws. "Quiche is served. Best you'll taste, in fact."

"And there we go." Rooster said.

~~~~~~~~~~~~~~~~~~~~~~~~~~~

The Witch of the East sat upright in her bed, jolted awake by a wave of magic.

Startled, she looked around her spacious, teal colored room. (Teal was this year's black in the East) None of the wards she had in place - at the door, three windows, two double doors to the balcony, and her secret escape door- were disturbed. It wasn't that she was expecting an assassination attempt, but from her own experience, she had found that it was always easier to kill people who weren't expecting it. So she always expected an assassination attempt even though she didn't expect it to happen.

Just in case.

The Witch swiveled around and slipped her feet into her teal colored, s'More fur slippers. "What just happened?" She stood and padded to a large mirror set between her balcony doors. When she got there, she smoothed her sleeping gown and her hair as she looked at her reflection. "Mirror, mirror on the wall... Wake up!"

Her reflection in the mirror shimmered then swirled away as if someone had dropped a rock into a clear pool. A grey face formed from the swirling. "Do you know what time it is?" As the face came into focus, so did the tasseled sleeping cap on his head.

"It's not that late." The Witch said. "Why are you even asleep? Do you even *need* to sleep?"

"Hey, I had a long day."

The pair stared at each other for a long moment.

"Well?" The Mirror asked.

The Witch looked over her shoulder at her bed. "I was just wondering..."

"Gads, woman," the Mirror said. "Yes, you're good looking. Even just out of bed. If I had appendages, even I'd show you a good time. Feel better?" He rolled his eyes. "And I thought my brother had it tough with that other Witch. 'Am I pretty?' He said in a high-pitched voice. "Prettiest of the pretty." His voice returned to normal. "Really, really super pretty?" He said in the falsetto again. "Oh yes," his voice deepened. "Prettiest of them all?" He high-pitched again. "I mean, honestly. Is that all you witches ever think about?"

168

"Listen..." Began the Witch, tersely.

"If you ask me, a little confidence would do you all some good."

"I was just..."

"I think you'd all be a bit happier just being content with your looks."

"Would you please..."

"Then you witches wouldn't be hiring loggers to cut the hearts out of young gals." He started. "Did you hear what I just said? *Cutting out young girls' hearts?* What kind of person even..."

"Can I just ask..."

"Listen, I get the being evil thing. It's a tough gig and you want to always be on the top of your game. Hashtag me too."

"Hash what?"

"Nothing." The Mirror said. He cleared his throat and recited:

> *Oh Witch of the East, your beauty is hard to deny-*
> *tight like a tiger. Like a panther; lithe.*

> *Many in the lands have more attributes tis true;*
> *hips that are wide, breasts that are huge.*

"Would you please just..."

> *But they're slugs. Soft as a newborn pup.*
> *When construction workers whistle at you, you beat them to a pulp.*

169

"Oh. Well..." A smile played across the Witch's face. She gave a small curtsy. "I do stay fit." She frowned. "But no, that's not it." She looked around the room. "Something's wrong."

"You miss a workout?"

"No!" She smiled again. "Of course not. It's just that something's wrong with the Magical Ether."

The face in the mirror looked down, then to his left. "Huh. Be right back." The face turned then moved out of view- the mirror returned to just being a mirror.

The Witch stood for a moment, hoping for a quick return. After a minute, she moved to her vanity and started brushing her hair.

Twenty minutes later, the Witch was doing sit-ups with her feet flat on the floor.

"Want me to wait for the end of the set?" The Mirror asked.

Since he had left, the Witch had combed her hair, completed whatever ablutions were required, and had changed into her exercise outfit- a tight fitting black leotard with a loose shirt over it.

"Eighty-nine," she said as she fell back. She lifted herself up and back down. "Ninety. Okay." She spun around on her butt to face the mirror.

"Just ninety?" The Mirror said with a smirk.

"Of my fourth set. Where'd you go?"

"Running down leads. Checking on things. Seeing who's who in the zoo."

"That's pretty vague."

"Well, I have my sources," the Mirror said noncommittally. "With non-attribution agreements and non-competition addendums... and such."

"And?"

"And..." The Mirror hesitated. "There's an issue."

"An issue?"

"It's more of an incident."

"An incident? What kind of incident?"

"An accident."

"Now it's an accident? Listen, just spit it out."

"Fine." The Mirror pursed its lips. "There's been murder."

The Witch leaned forward, elbows on her knees, she grabbed her feet. "Oh no! Not..." Panic surged through her- if the Witch of the West was dead, then she was without any ally at all and the conniving Witch of the North would move to get rid of her next. It was a power play she had been expecting for years. Ever since the visitor from afar arrived and declared himself a Wizard, forcing uneasy alliances.

"No." The Mirror looked to his left then forward. "It's the snow queen."

"She murdered someone?" She got to her feet.

"She was on the receiving end, it seems."

The Witch breathed a sigh of relief. "Oh." It seemed odd that the Witch of the South was killed- neither she nor her sister from the west had any plans to eliminate the other two witches. At least officially anyway. "What happened?"

"Someone poisoned her."

The Witch scrunched up her face. "Poison? That's a coward's tool. Do you know who did it?"

"Coward might be a strong word."

"Who else would use an underhanded...."

"A stupid rooster." The Mirror smiled. "It's ironic actually, seeing as how she avoided all meats, to be killed by a delicious white meat."

The Witch snickered. "Okay, that is kind of ironic. But how did a rooster even get to where he could add meat to her meal?" She shook her head, "This wouldn't have happened if she ate a balanced diet. Took care of herself more."

"Do you want you hear the 'they are slugs' poem again?"

The Witch laughed. "That's okay. So where did this rooster come from?"

"Run of the mill rooster is what I hear. But he's traveling with a Munchkin, some goat, and a young man." The Mirror hesitated. "Uhm..."

"What's wrong?"

"The young man is from the same place as... *him*."

"What? When did he show up? Does anyone else know?"

The Mirror looked off to his left again, unsure of how to answer.

"Well?" The Witch stomped her foot. "Who else knows? *Everyone*?"

"I'm sure there are plenty of folks around that don't know current events," the Mirror said noncommittally.

"Everyone then."

"No, no. Not everyone." The Mirror chuckled. "Of course, not everyone."

"Who doesn't know?"

"The Wizard, as far as I can tell, has no clue."

"That's a daily occurrence for him, the dolt. But the other witches know."

"You didn't until a moment ago."

"The *other* witches!"

"I'm afraid so."

"Come on! What do I pay you for?"

"I'm a slave trapped in this mirror; you don't pay me anything." The Mirror smiled. "Are you going to start?"

"Well," the Witch said uncomfortably, "it's just an expression."

"I see." The Mirror answered as his smile faded.

"And who does this rooster work for? The Blue Witch?"

"I can't see how your friend in the North could be involved." The Mirror lied.

"And her talisman?"

The Mirror didn't make eye contact. "I wasn't aware that the Witch of the North had a talisman. I thought she only had her wand and those bubbles of hers."

The Witch stomped forward, crowding the Mirror. "You know what I mean!"

"The young man has it." The Mirror said. "Apparently."

"And I imagine they are heading north now. To bring it to her!" She whirled and moved to her vanity quickly. "We will just see about that!"

"Now don't go making rush decisions," the Mirror said. "Best to think things over and be deliberate. The castle of the Witch of the South is vulnerable right now; no one there even knows she's gone. And as such, no one there had made any sort of decision regarding the matter. The last thing they need is you going off half-cocked down there." The Mirror sighed. "You... We need a plan to deal with this accident."

"This was no *accident*. It was a deliberate killing of that stupid snow-bound witch by the scheming Witch of the North." She reached down and grabbed a pair of ruby encrusted slippers. "And the odds are that I'm next on the death list of that bubble floating bimbo." She slipped a shoe on her foot, then grabbing it near the heel, she pulled up on the sides of the shoe. The shoe pulled up almost to her knee, forming a tight, knee-high ruby boot. She pulled the other one the same way. "Well two can play at that game." She stood akimbo. "I've got a score to settle with that Witch."

"I suppose..."

"And I play every game to win."

"Why keep score if you're not playing to win." The Mirror said, repeating the saying on one of the many posters in the Witch's workout room.

"Exactly!" The Witch of the East rubbed her hands together. "So, I'm going to go up there and confront that bimbo!"

"I think it would be best to see what's going on down south first."

The Witch pursed her lips. "Hmmm. Okay. I'll hop down there and see what the servants have to say about recent events."

174

"Remember they don't suspect anything so don't tip your hand. The Witch of the North isn't going anywhere; you can visit her any time."

"Keep an eye on her." The Witch clapped her hands once, dispelling the Djin that she had entrapped in her mirror. She stomped to her closet and pulled out a long black cape. With a twirl, she spun it around her and clasped it at her neck. She flipped the cloak back, revealing a ruby lining. "Roosters and Munchkins, and Goats? Wait till they get a load of me."

She moved to the window even though the magic worked no matter where she stood. "Castle of the Witch of the South," she said as she clicked her heels together. "Castle of the Witch of the South." She clicked her heels again. The room around her shimmered as if she were entering a dream. "Castle of the Witch of the South!" She clicked her heels a third time and her surroundings swirled and shifted.

~~~~~~~~~~~~~~~~~~~~~~~~~~~

Marren frowned as he looked over the side of the wagon. His chin was resting on a side board and his feet dangled down.

"What's wrong?" Honus asked. He had been sitting in the back of the wagon, looking to the side but now he moved to the back beside the man so they were both on the back of the wagon facing the way they had come.

Unable to say that he was upset that he had missed his chance to gain possession of the talisman he opted for something he knew they could both agree on: "That stupid rooster running the show."

Honus looked over his shoulder. Gertie was holding the reins to the donkey pulling the cart. Rooster was sound asleep beside her. They had barely ridden out of the castle walls before he

175

had fallen asleep. Honus smiled. "At least he's quiet right now."

"I suppose." Marren said with a smirk. "We're heading north, huh? So that blue witch can send you home."

Honus looked down at the star pendant around his neck. "Do you think... really think that blue lady can get me home?"

"Witch." Marren corrected.

"Witch," Honus said. "It's hard to think that way; we don't have witches or magic back home."

"Home sounds boring."

Honus nodded. "Sometimes it is. Sometimes I feel like I'm going to jump out of my own skin if I don't get out of there."

Now Marren smiled. "Ahh, the age-old 'rooftops are yellower on the other side of the fence' dilemma."

"I think it's grass."

Marren glanced up at him. "Grass on a roof? That would leak. Thatch is the way to go."

"No," Honus smirked. "The saying where I come from is 'the grass is always greener on the other side of the fence'."

"Well, that's the same sentiment even though grass is always the same color green." He chuckled. "Around here anyway." Marren got serious. "Listen Honus, if you feel you should be someplace else, you should go someplace else."

"What?"

"What is it you are jumping out of your skin to do?"

"Play baseball. I am good at it. Great even. I know I could make a life playing."

"Then that's what you should do." Marren put his hand on the young man's shoulder. "Honus..."

"Walter." Honus interrupted. "Walter Johnson."

"What?"

Honus sighed. "My name isn't Honus. Or Barney. Or any of the other names I tell people. I just..."

"Listen. Whatever name you use, you need to follow your dream or you'll regret it. Believe me; I know all about regrets."

"What do you regret?"

Marren looked out the way they had come for a long while. Only the squeaking of the wheels broke the silence. "Not expressing my feelings to a woman when I had the chance."

"Did she marry someone else?"

"No."

"Then you can still tell her, right?"

Marren glanced at the talisman as it hung around Honus' neck. "It would take more than that, I think. It's complicated." He looked up at Honus. "Women, my young friend, in case you have not discovered, are complicated."

"Yeah." Honus thought back to the several girls he had dated. "I've discovered that."

"Then go follow your dream with this baseball game." He glanced at the talisman again. "Do it before it's too late, Honus."

Honus put his hand on the talisman. "Would... this help you? With that woman?"

"It would, yes." Marren said honestly.

"Then when I get home, take it. Unless it's that blue witch."

177

Marren shuddered. "Gads no. It's not her." He twirled a finger around his ear. "She's nuts, that one."

"I'm not one to judge."

"Thanks." Marren reached out and touched the talisman. An electric shock ran through him, making him flinch.

"It only does that when you first pick it up."

"That's good to hear." Marren shook his hand. He looked out the back of the wagon. "We'll get you home, then I'll go find my lady friend."

"Who is it, if you don't mind me asking."

"She's a farm girl," Marren lied. "Lives a village over from me. Her parents don't approve of me." He tapped the talisman. It zapped his fingers again. "This will let us move away and live our own lives together."

"Is she a real witch?"

"What? That's a thing to say!" Marren said, worried the youth had figured out who he was interested in.

Honus held up his hands. "I don't mean offence. It just seems that there are a lot of witches around here, is all."

"Oh." Marren chuckled. "So, Walter, huh?"

"Walter Johnson, actually."

"Maybe we'll just stick with Honus as a nickname to not be confusing. When you get back home, you can go by your real name."

"Okay."

"Okay."

The pair looked at the forest as they rode through it for a long while.

178

Gertie finally broke the silence: "What would be the odds of one of you actually doing something useful? Like steering this wagon?"

The two men looked at each other.

"Don't everyone volunteer at once."

Honus worked his way to his feet. "Sorry Gertie, I can do that."

"It's nice to see there is at least one gentleman here."

Marren worked his way to his feet also. "We'll take the reins, you can come back here and enjoy the scenery." He gestured around them. "We've got lots of it, it seems."

Gertie let go of the reins and hopped to the back of the wagon, crowding the two men. "That's fine by me. You two sit with that annoying bird."

Honus stepped over Gertie and onto the bench. "He's asleep; how can he be annoying?" He sat beside Rooster.

Rooster kicked him as his feet twitched.

"Okay, that's a little annoying." Honus said. "As long as he doesn't fart too." He looked down at Rooster.

"You still saying things like that?" Marren worked his way onto the bench beside Honus. "What's the matter with you?" He leaned forward and looked around Honus at Rooster. "If he starts farting, you're in deep trouble."

"I don't think chickens *can* far." Honus said. "I've never heard one do it, anyway."

"You sit around listening for chicken farts?" Marren laughed.

"No. I mean, I did spend a bit of time in chicken coops if that's worth anything."

"You were a chicken wrangler?"

"I lived in one for three months just to get off the streets."

"Oh." Marren looked uncomfortable. "Sorry."

Honus smiled. "Don't be. It was better than getting rained on." Now he laughed. "And when the rooster crowed, I'd sneak out so the farmer had no idea I was there. That rooster was a great alarm clock."

"Three months?"

Honus shrugged. "Yeah. I was there until I got into the house I'm in now. Got a bed and everything."

"That's good to hear." Marren took the reins as he leaned back. He snapped the reins. "Keep moving donkey."

The donkey turned and brayed at him.

"Finally." Honus said.

"What?"

"That's the first animal that has acted like I expected it to."

"I'm glad to oblige you," the Donkey answered. He turned and looked forward again.

Marren elbowed Honus playfully.

"Of course, it can talk." Honus sighed. "At least we're heading north with the talisman. I feel bad for that witch back there though. I can't believe we got away with it."

Marren elbowed Honus harder. "You're doing it again."

"Sorry." Honus looked up at the canopy of trees. "Nothing's happened so we're okay, I suppose."

"Oh boy." Marren muttered. "Here we go." He snapped the reins. "Pick up the pace, Mister Donkey; we're probably going to have company."

~~~~~~~~~~~~~~~~~~~~~~~~~~

The Witch of the East shimmered into existence in the massive foyer of the Witch of the South's castle several minutes after she had left.

A bored-looking youth startled as she appeared. He stood up behind the table he was sitting behind and picked up a trombone. "Welcome..." He paused as he looked to figure out who had arrived. "Witch of the East!" He blew the trombone, pulling and pushing the slide to form notes.

"Yes, thanks..."

The youth continued to blow the trombone, working the slide as he did. A tune started to form.

The Witch of the East put her hands on her hips. "If you would..."

The youth continued to play, eyes rolling around as if he were keeping an eye out for someone.

"How much longer..."

The youth leaned back as he hit a particularly high note.

"Of all the..."

The youth held the note for almost ten seconds. When he lowered the trombone, he smiled wide at the Witch of the East.

"Yes. Very nice."

The youth took a bow. "Thanks. I usually don't get to finish the song; the Mistress of the Castle usually shows up and yells at me." He looked around. "Weird."

"Maybe she's busy dealing with other matters?" The Witch of the South said, noncommittally. "Elsewhere?"

"Didn't know she had left the castle, Miss." The youth brought the trombone back to his lips.

"Oh. That's not necessary. Please."

The youth played several notes then smiled. "That should do it."

The Witch of the East casually looked over her shoulder. The monstrous wooden doors were bolted shut. "Do what?"

An ape lumbered into the room. "What racket about?"

The youth pointed at the Witch with his trombone. "The esteemed Witch of the East is here for a visit."

"I was just passing by," the Witch lied. "Popped in to give my regards is all."

The ape turned to the youth. "She out."

The youth looked at the Witch. "The Mistress of the Castle is not available, I am afraid."

"Went to see that western dame." The ape said to the youth.

"I can hear what..."

"The Mistress of the Castle has gone to see her associate, the venerated Witch of the West regarding matters of magic."

"I see. So perhaps when she..." The Witch of the East began.

"Not sure when she come back." Interrupted the ape.

"Apparently she will be away for an indeterminate amount of time," the youth relayed.

"That's getting annoying," the Witch said. "Can I wait perhaps?"

"Nope." The ape said. "Rules is rules."

"It is with deepest sympathy honored Witch of the East that we must decline your offer."

The Witch put her hands back on her hips. "Listen."

"Mistress out, no one about." The ape said.

"We couldn't properly receive someone of your high social stature while the mistress of the castle is out."

"Listen," the Witch snapped. "I don't need you fluffing up what that ape says. I just wanted to wait here for a little bit." She gave a sweet smile. "Can't you just bend the rules a little?"

"Sign the sheet, get a treat." Reminded the ape.

"Our employment contract specifically states that we are to follow the rules of the castle at all times to ensure a pleasant employment."

"Can I maybe visit with any other guests you have?"

"Bust a deal. Ride the wheel," warned the ape.

The youth nodded at the ape. He had seen castle servants strapped to the large wooden gristmill wheel. It wasn't pretty. "There is really no way we can allow you to stay, acclaimed Witch of the East. It would pain me greatly if you did."

The ape nodded. Because it would.

The Witch put out her lower lip slightly.

"Honestly, Miss; I'm running out of synonyms." Admitted the youth. "Please just come back tomorrow; she'll be back by then, I'm sure."

"Fine, fine." The Witch said. "I'll come back later."

"Later, lady." The ape waved.

"Excellent." The youth nodded. "You are most welcome to visit when the Mistress of the Castle returns."

The Witch snorted a laugh then caught herself. "That's never."

"What?"

The Witch blanched. "Oh... well... you know well enough that your Mistress of the Castle and I don't see eye to eye on a lot of things, so 'welcome' is a strong word. Tolerate is more like it."

"It's not my place to talk about such things." The youth said. He held up the trombone. "I just announce folks."

"She think you conniving hag." The ape said flatly. "Want her dead."

Now the young man paled. "I'm not sure I would put it that way, estee... venera.... really fit Witch of the East."

"Yes. Well. I'll be going then." The Witch hesitated when she realized she hadn't brought her broom along. The ruby shoes were great for covering large distances in a very short amount of time, but they were impractical for just moving around an area or a town. She decided to just walk out so she turned and faced the massive wood door. "Does this open or is it just for show?" She snapped.

"Nighttime is closed time." The ape said.

"Unfortunately errr... Miss, the portcullis doesn't get opened at night."

184

She turned back around. "So how do you propose I leave?"

"Sooner better than later?" Offered the ape.

"The same way you came?" The youth tried. "If at all possible."

The Witch of the East frowned then whispered "The Crossroads." She clicked her heels together. "The Crossroads." She clicked them again.

"Not fast way to travel." The ape observed.

Overcoming the urge to address the ape which would cause the shoes to overheat and not work for an embarrassing ten minutes, the Witch instead whispered a third time 'the Crossroads' as she clicked her heels once more.

The Witch's view of the door shimmered and shifted to a dark forest only several seconds later since it was only a short distance away. She turned in a quick circle to get her bearings. The yellow brick road under her feet branched off in three directions.

"Hey there." A voice said.

The Witch ignored it. She looked back towards the castle of the Witch of the South- it was almost five miles away but clearly visible on its snowy mountain.

"Hey, you."

"I really need to see about adjusting these shoes." She said to no one in particular.

The magic embued in the shoes allowed her to travel almost instantly to anywhere she had previously gone, or to a prominent geographical location. They could also dispel most any magical spell no matter how lethal. The main issue with them was that the magic wasn't exact- going to the castle of the Witch of the South took her to the main entrance. Going to the Emerald City or MudSling City would also take her to their main gates. She did not have a way to target a particular room in a castle, or city unless she had been to that exact location and could articulate it- 'down by the river bend' would not work, however 'the fishing shack at the river bend' would. She stared at the illuminated upper rooms of the castle trying to figure out a way to transport herself there. Without her broom, it might as well have been a thousand miles away. "Damned annoying."

"Can you help with a little nail bending?"

She crossed her arms and continued to stare at the castle.

"Got a minute?"

The Witch of the East turned to face the scarecrow positioned in a field of corn on the other side of a white fence. "What? What, what *what*?!?"

"You want to get me off this pole?"

"I want to set you afire."

The scarecrow looked left and right, judging the distance to the next corn row and potential freedom. It was pretty close. "Want to take me off this pole first?"

The Witch stared at the scarecrow. "Nope."

"Never mind then." The scarecrow said, deciding he would wait for someone less magical, and hopefully more gullible to get him down. "Forget I said anything."

"Home, home, home", the Witch said as she clicked her heels. The dark forest shifted to her bedroom. She looked at the mirror- seeing only herself. With a tired sigh, she turned and walked to her bed and flopped down on it, face down. It was, after all, the middle of the night. "Tomorrow. Tomorrow I'll figure out where they are."

186

"Have we figured out where we are?" Honus asked.

"We are heading north, of course," Rooster said. He had moved to the back of the wagon.

"None of this looks familiar to me," Marren said. "I hope you didn't get us lost while you were up her."

Rooster pointed with his wing towards the rising sun. "We're going North, I tell you. Due. North."

"The sun comes up in the East," Honus said. "Everyone knows that."

"Not everyone," Marren observed. "Listen, Rooster..."

"Listen to the sun coming up in the North?" Rooster held a wing up to his ear. "Ahh."

"Listen, Rooster..."

"Shhh! I'm listening to the sun rising, Munchkin." He tilted his head as he listened. "Seems the sun says we're heading north and..." He leaded forward a little. "And the sun says I'm the smartest one in this wagon."

"You're not even the smartest *bird* in the wagon."

The donkey shook his head as he continued to walk.

"Who told you the sun rose in the North?" Honus asked, taking a different approach.

"Everyone knows that."

"But... Who told you?"

Rooster dropped his wings and turned to face Honus. "Ever seen a map?"

"Sure," Honus answered.

"And which way was up?"

"Oh boy," Gertie said. "I know where this is going."

"Say it, Honus," Marren said. "Might as well get it over with."

"North is up." Honus said flatly.

Rooster pointed at the sun. "And where is the Sun going right now?"

Honus shook his head. "Up," he said, meekly.

Rooster took a bow. "I rest my case."

"You're an idiot," Marren said.

"A complete buffoon." Gertie added.

Rooster stood tall, spreading his wings. "Any time you want to dance, little man! You and your little goat, too!"

"Everyone just calm down," Honus said.

"If I may make a comment," Donkey said.

Rooster pecked at the air. "The chickens have come home to roost and you're going to reap the whirlwind!"

"That doesn't even make sense," Marren said. "Maybe I can knock some sense into you." He balled up his fists.

"Excuse me," Donkey said.

"Everyone just calm down!" Honus said.

"You first, little man!" Rooster did a little hop.

The donkey brayed loudly. "Hey!"

"That's as good as a bell." Rooster jumped onto Marren, hitting him with his wings.

188

Gertie pushed past Honus, knocking him into the back of the wagon. "Let me at him!"

~~~~~~~~~~~~~~~~~~~~~~~~~~~~~~

The Witch of the East sat up in bed and stretched. "What a terrible night." She looked over at the large grandfather clock- it was almost ten.

A rooster crowed somewhere outside.

The witch smirked. "I'm not the only one sleeping in, it seems." She slipped out of bed.

A donkey brayed angrily somewhere outside.

"I really need to get the stables moved," she remarked to no one in particular as she padded to her vanity. She picked up a brush and ran it through her long black hair. "Why I even let them put it there at the front of the castle is beyond me."

A goat bleated angrily somewhere outside.

"Sooner rather than later." The witch put the brush down.

A donkey brayed angrily somewhere outside- again.

"Come on, it's early still." The witch stood and started toward the bathroom, hoping that by the time she was out, the ruckus outside would be over.

A man shouted loudly somewhere outside the window.

The witch turned and walked to the window, hands hovering in front of the curtains.

Someone cursed loudly somewhere outside. In Munchkin.

"What?" The witch pushed the curtains aside and looked. A mere hundred yards away on the road that led directly to the castle, a small wagon rocked back and forth because a

189

Munchkin was grappling with a rooster while a goat pulled on the seat of the Munchkin's pants as a young man tried to pick up the goat which only lifted the back end of the Munchkin causing the rooster's head to bang against the floorboard each time the entire sequence occurred. "A rooster, a munchkin, and a goat, oh my." She said as she watched. It was mesmerizing. And a little entertaining.

Even so, after the fifth iteration of the rooster's head banging on the wood, the witch opened the window. "Hey!" She shouted -partially to the occupants of the wagon, but even more so to the guards at the front of the castle that were watching the spectacle instead of doing something about it. "Stop that!"

"Now you've done it," the donkey said. "That's one unhappy witch."

"Witch?" Rooster said. "Did you say..."

"You idiot," Marren hissed. "Look where you led us!"

"Everyone calm down," Honus said. "Let's just see about turning the wagon and getting out of here." He looked at the donkey. "Mister Donkey, if you could please..."

"What are you doing in my lands?" The Witch shouted.

"Oh boy," Honus said. "She does sound angry."

"This is private property, not your personal wrestling arena!"

"Sorry!" Honus shouted back. "We'll just..."

The witch gestured at the guards that were finally moving forward. "Bring them inside!"

"That's not good," Gertie said as she let go of Marren's pants.

Honus let go of Gertie. "I say we make a run for it."

190

The donkey shook his head. "No way I'm going to get away from guards on horseback and flying monkeys." A thought occurred to him. "But if you'll just unhitch me, that might help."

"You want us to all ride you bareback?" Honus said.

"No, what I want is... sure, that's it. Just unhitch me first."

"Come with me," a guard said as he took Donkey's harness. "Let's go donkey." He turned and started toward the castle.

"You know, we'd love to go with you," Marren said as sat on the side rail of the wagon, "but we've got an important appointment we need to get to. We really can't miss it."

"I didn't realize the Idiots Guild was meeting this week," the guard said without even looking back.

"Nice," Rooster said. He looked at Honus. "You want to feed him a straight line next or..." His eyes fell to the star pendant prominently displayed around his neck. "Ixnay on the eclace nay."

"What?"

"Ide hay the ecklace nay." Rooster said.

"I don't understand what you're saying," Honus answered.

Marren pointed. "Get that necklace hidden, boy; that thing is a hot commodity right now," he whispered.

"Oh no!" He tucked it into his shirt then looked down at his chest. "That's the first place she'll look!"

"Swallow it," Rooster said.

"What?"

"Yeah, swallow it. Then in eight to ten hours, you'll get it back." Rooster said.

191

"I recommend a lot of bread and corn to go along with it."
Marren grimaced. "That's got some pointy ends on it; you'll
probably choke to death. Just stick it up your butt and save the
swallowing."

"I'm not going to swallow it." Honus said. He took the
talisman off.

"Up the butt then." Marren nodded. "Good move."

"I'm not going to..."

"Hide it in the wagon," Gertie suggested.

Honus looked around the wagon- it was just a bare bones,
simple wagon. "Where?"

Rooster pointed with his wing. "We're almost there. Swallow
it."

"Stick it up your butt." Marren said.

"I'm not sticking it up my butt," Honus said. "What's the
matter with you?"

"Then swallow it."

"Hide it in the wagon!"

"Up the butt."

"You know I can hear you talking, right?" The guard said. "I
really don't want to, but unfortunately I can."

Honus pulled his pants out and dropped the talisman down the
front of his pants. He grimaced as it shocked him. "There."

"That's the second place she'll look," Marren remarked. He
smiled. "If you're lucky."

"Now you'll need to wash it before you swallow it." Rooster
cocked his head to the side. "And afterwards, of course."

The wagon stopped in front of the castle.

As the massive portcullis slowly lifted out of the way the guard turned to face the wagon. "No weapons allowed inside the grounds."

"I have a rapier wit," Rooster said. "I'll just stay behind with it. How's that sound?"

"If you use it, I'll blunt your head." The guard said. "How's that sound?"

"Deal." Marren said. He jerked a thumb at the guard. "I'm starting to like this guy."

"If I could frown, I would." Rooster said. He squatted down. "I'll settle for sitting quietly and sulking."

"Whose castle is this?" Honus asked. "If you don't mind me asking, that is."

"This is the castle of the most powerful, benevolent, and honorable Witch of the East." The guard said as the portcullis finally reached its top.

"No beating around the bush with this one, huh?" Rooster commented.

"Do we have to go in?" Honus gestured at his compatriots. "We really do have someplace else to be." He looked up. "And we'd like to get there before dark."

"Shhh." Marren said.

"And where would that be?" The guard asked.

"Quiet," Marren warned.

"Errr..." Honus said, unsure now how much he should tell the guard. He tugged on his crotch. He hoped subtly.

"Ur?" The guard smirked. "That's a great deal farther than a day from here."

"What?"

"Ancient far off land. Used to be right on the ocean but now it's miles inland?" The Guard pointed westward. "That way, if my geography is right."

"No, it's not... that.... exactly..."

"Well, while you figure out where you're going, you can go see the Esteemed Witch of the East."

"Just let it go," Gertie said.

"Let it go?" Honus said.

"Yes; this witch never bothered me anyway."

"Oooh!" Marren perked up. "Oooh!"

The guard pointed at the Munchkin. "Stop right there. We'll have none of that." He started walking, pulling donkey with him. "Not while I'm on shift."

"So, we're to just have the sound of silence?" Marren tried. Hopefully.

"Stop." The guard ordered.

Honus scratched at his crotch. He hoped unobtrusively.

Marren frowned. "Fine then."

"Oh boy." Honus said. He shifted his hips left and right then in a little circle.

The guard raised an eyebrow at Honus.

"Come on, guard," Rooster said. "There's lines being tossed left and right here. It's not fair I can't take a swing once and a while."

The guard pulled the wagon to a large oak door. "Fine. Just be judicious about it. The mistress does not appreciate too much humor."

"A rare wit, then?" Rooster said.

"Oh boy." The guard pulled the large door open. "She is by far the most level headed and calm and composed of any of the witches living in our fair lands."

"Than the other three?" Honus asked.

"You think there's only three witches living around here?" The guard asked, honestly perplexed.

"Yes?"

"Oooh! Oooh!" Rooster rose his wing. "Tag me in!"

"Well, I just figured since that's what folks talked about, that's all there was. I mean, how many witches do you need?"

"Meee!" Rooster did a little hop.

The guard looked at Rooster. "He always like this?"

"Sometimes better," admitted Rooster.

Honus scratched his crotch.

"Let's just get in there, say hello to your esteemed level headed calm composed witch of yours so we can get going," Gertie said.

"Don't rush her," warned the guard.

"Or what?" Rooster cocked his head to the side.

The guard opened the door. "Follow me." He started down the narrow passage.

"Or what?" Honus asked.

The guard stopped and turned to face the group. "Are you asking 'or what' to me asking you to follow me or to why you shouldn't rush any woman, or a witch for that matter. Much less the Witch of the East in her own castle?"

Honus stomped a foot as a jolt of electricity ran down his leg.

"Lead the way." Rooster said.

"We're going to need Lady Luck to smile on us," Marren said, "to get out of this predicament."

"We'll need more than a smile," Rooster said to him. "She's going to have to hike up her skirt, I think."

Honus took a step when another bolt of energy shot out of the star. "Ahh!" He said as his right leg went stiff. He hobbled behind the group. "Oooh!" He said, even though it didn't help with the shocks he was receiving.

"Is he okay?" The guard asked Marren. "I mean, he seems like he has issues and witch or not, the mistress of the castle is still a lady and I don't feel comfortable having her witness his antics."

Marren and the guard turned to look at Honus. He was walking on his toes.

"He's not from around here," Marren tried as he fell in step behind the guard. "His ways are different than ours?"

Honus stomped his feet. "Gah!" He said as he tugged down on his pant leg. Near his crotch.

"They sure are." The guard pointed. "Let's go. She does not like to be kept waiting."

~~~~~~~~~~~~~~~~~~~~~~~~~~~

"Stall them!" The Witch of the East said to her valet.

"Ma'am?" The elderly man said.

"There're rumors that the Witch of the South is dead."

"I've heard. Most unfortunate."

"And she was killed by a rooster."

"Most unusual." The valet observed. "That is not the traditional weapon of choice to assassinate someone. And this is an issue because... the Witch of the South is dead?"

"Well, sort of. I mean, the killing of a coven member dictates that we, the remaining members, avenge her death."

"But..."

"But my sources tell me that that stupid frost queen was looking at offing all of us sooner rather than later."

The valet smirked. "And..."

"And there were plans put in place by certain parties in this room to do that same thing to her."

The valet nodded. "Another month and it would have been done, Ma'am." He shrugged. "But to have an outsider do it? Bad form that. And it sets a bad precedent."

"Exactly." The witch scowled. "Do your own dirty work."

"If you don't mind me asking, Ma'am, why is this an issue right now? This morning."

The Witch pointed toward the window. "There's a rooster out there right now. This morning."

"Huh."

"Yeah." She looked toward the window. "I'm having them brought in. See who they're working for."

"Bringing assassins... especially unaffiliated, not even on the payroll assassins into the castle can be dangerous." The man pointed downward. "Might I suggest one of the outer rooms? Outside the inner defenses?"

"That does sound prudent. Take them to the Zen Room. I'll be right there."

"Where are you going?"

"To talk to that stupid blue witch. She has to be behind this."

"If she is, then going there might not be wise, if you don't mind me saying. You should be careful."

The witch walked to her vanity and opened a drawer. "I'll be careful." She removed a long, black, twisted blade. "And make sure I don't hit a rib."

"Ahh. Right then." The valet turned. "I will corral the guests to the Zen Room." He looked over his shoulder. "Refreshments?"

"They aren't staying that long." She slipped the dagger into the top of her now thigh-high ruby boots then grabbed the broom leaning against the vanity.

"Where are you going, if you don't mind me asking?"

The Witch clicked her heels. A smile came to her face. "Private Balcony of the Witch of the North."

"Very well then." The valet stopped to watch from the door as the witch repeated herself two more times and disappeared. He shook his head. The plan was for the witches of the east and west to be dispatched first, then the southern one. Then, once the coven was down to just one, the issue of the wizard would be dealt with. By force if necessary. "Good thing I always get my payment in advance." He put on a fake smile as he left to go meet what had to be a cold and calculating assassin. Rooster or not, if he had been able to dispatch the strongest witch of the Cardinal Coven all on his own, the reports of him being incompetent had to be incorrect.

~~~~~~~~~~~~~~~~~~~~~~~~~~~

The Blue Witch leaned precariously over the railing as she searched over her map for any other magical disturbances. Yet another eruption of ruby bubbles let her know the Witch of the East was on the move again. "Busy little dung beetle, aren't we my pretty!" She said. She scanned the map to see where the witch would reappear. When ruby bubbles sizzled right over her own castle a few seconds later, she righted herself. "Paying a visit, how undelightful."

With a flourish of her lounging gown, she moved to the door and opened it. Since the demise of the witch of the south, there was now a guard in her main room. "We have visitors."

"We do?" The guard looked around the room. "Here?"

"No, not here, you idiot. I mean at the front of the castle." She raised her hand as if she were deciding whether to slap the guard. "Get word to the castle gate that no one... *no one* is to enter."

"Enter here or the castle in general?"

The Witch balled up her fist, now deciding whether to round-house him or just give him a hearty jab. "The castle!"

"I'm just trying to make sure I understand who I'm supposed to stop and where."

"What?"

"I'm just trying..." He started again. "Huh." Then he pointed. "What about that?" The guard was pointing over the Witch's shoulder.

Silhouetted against the window was a figure. It seemed to be leaning against the balustrade of her balcony and holding a pole.

"Want me to deal with...this issue first?"

The Witch of the North shook her head. "No, I know who it is." She moved to the double doors leading to the balcony. "Just stay sharp." With that, she yanked both doors open, revealing the Witch of the East.

"Ahh, Miss E," The Witch of the North said, combining the other witch's name and location- something she knew the other witch did not like. At all.

The Witch of the East tightened her grip on her broom at the jab. So she returned the favor: "I don't have time for games, *Bubbles*."

~~Bubbles~~ The Witch of the North raised the stakes: "So where you keeping Mombi? Under your stairs?"

"She's not in my spandrel," she answered, using the actual term for the space located under stairs when there is not another set immediately below them. "You should read more and huff from your caldron less." She looked the other up and down. "And maybe lift a weight or two once and a while." She shifted her weight onto her broom and smirked. "Then maybe you'd be able to fly without an industrial sized bubble around you."

The guard in the room gasped. He brought his shield up, expecting fireworks. Lethal ones.

The Witch of the North took a step back from the stinging insults. Especially the second one. "They are called curves. Men like them."

The guard ducked behind his shield.

"So, you had the Witch of the South killed." The Witch of the East said, cutting to the chase.

"I did no such thing. It seems a rooster did it all on his own."

"How do you know it was a rooster?" The Witch of the East picked up her broom. "If you weren't involved."

"Everyone who is anyone knows." Now the Witch of the North smirked. "Maybe if you'd spend less time picking up weights and looking at your butt in a mirror, you could set up a decent informant network."

The Witch of the East swung her leg over her broom, exposing a toned leg as she tossed her cape to the other side. "This isn't over."

"Get. Off. My. Balcony." The Witch of the North seethed. "Before I drop a house on you to see if you can pick that up!"

Without a reply, the Witch leaned over the balustrade, falling heels over head over the side.

The Witch of the North moved to the railing quickly but by the time she looked down, the other witch had flown off.

"Wow," the Guard said.

Fuming, the Witch of the North turned. "Wow, what? Wow; that was bold to come to my private balcony and accuse me of wrongdoings? Or wow; that's pretty rude to make a comment about someone's physique? Or wow; that witch doesn't know who she's dealing with and it's going to get her killed?"

Without thinking the guard replied. "Wow; nice legs." He caught himself. "No, I mean that second one! Definitely that second one!" He hesitated. "And the third one?"

The Witch jabbed a suddenly long and crooked finger at the guard. "Hah!" She incanted.

The guard didn't answer.

Because he was a toadstool.

"I'll get her if it's the last thing I do!" The Witch said as she kicked the toadstool into bits. "Her and her sulfur stinking sister!"

~~~~~~~~~~~~~~~~~~~~~~~~

The valet straightened his vest as he stood in front of the ornately carved door. After a second deep breath, he put a diplomatic smile on his face, eased the door open and entered the room.

It was a disaster.

A young man was standing on an end table that had been set atop a coffee table, scratching its inlaid wood top. Both had been pushed against the floor to ceiling bookcases that lined three walls of the room. A massive fireplace took up the far end. The young man was jumping up and trying to grab a rooster. Causing more scratches to the coffee table.

A Munchkin picked up a book (from the many strewn on the floor) and threw it at the rooster.

It hit the young man in the back then fell to the ground sending several pages flying.

The valet stepped into the center of the room "What is going on? Those are first editions!"

A vase whizzed by the valet's head shattering against the bookcase very close to the rooster.

He turned to look. A goat was shifting sideways, looking over her shoulder as she sighted ostensibly at the rooster. Another vase was directly behind her back legs. "Those are antiques!"

The valet shouted. He picked up the vase before the goat could kick it. "They are from the Third Ozmanian Dynasty!" He turned the vase upside down and looked at its base. "Fifteen hundred twenty-five!"

"All of you are fired!" The rooster shouted.

The Valet wheeled around to look at the rooster. He was prancing along the bookshelf, kicking books off to make room as he went. A golden colored star medallion hung from his neck.

"Fired, I tell you!" The rooster looked down at the Valet. "Nice; a servant. Get this riffraff out of here!" He pointed with his wing. "Starting with that little runt!"

"Hey now," Marren said, "that's getting personal."

"That's impossible; you're not a person; you're a runt!" The rooster said. He rubbed the medallion, "And you're not getting my treasure."

Still trying to be diplomatic, the Valet stepped between the pair. "A wise doctor once said 'a person is a person, no matter how small'."

"Listen you servant..." The rooster said. "I said I wanted these hoodlums gone, so make it happen."

"I'm the Valet," the Valet corrected.

Rooster cocked his head to the side. "That's odd; if the owner of this castle is a witch, why aren't you a handmaiden?"

"I am the butler of this estate and I act as the valet to its owner. There are no female staff, hence the need for a butler." The Valet said matter-of-factly. "Now get off that shelf." He pointed at the ground. "You Sir, are making a mockery of this noble room."

Rooster flapped to the ground. "Huh."

203

Honus looked down at the man, seemingly only now realizing where he was standing. "Oh, I am sorry." He hopped down and picked up the end table. There were numerous deep gouges in the coffee table. "Oh no. I don't know what came over me." He put the table down near where he had originally picked it up then returned for the coffee table. "I'm so sorry."

The valet smiled. "I will have the room serviced young man. For now, let's just all calm down and..."

A Third Ozmanian Dynasty vase - this one from fifteen hundred twenty-eight, shattered against the Valet's head.

As the man crumpled to the ground, Marren leapt forward and yanked the talisman off Rooster's neck.

"Hey, that's mine!" Rooster said.

Marren pulled his leg back, preparing to kick the bird. "You stupid bird! You got us captured by the very witch we were trying to avoid!"

"And I got us uncaptured," Gertie said. "Let's get going before someone really important shows up." She started for the door. "Move it!"

"Well, as butler, he was in charge of all goings on in the castle, so he was pretty important," Rooster observed.

Gertie head-butted the door open. "Leave him if he doesn't want to go."

Honus put his hand out for the talisman. "Thanks, Marren."

Marren hesitated.

"Thanks, Marren," Honus said again. He held his hand out farther.

Marren tossed the talisman, knowing he could get it back later. Easily. "Yeah, let's get going."

"Follow me," Gertie said as she exited the room, Honus close behind.

Marren did a small detour to the fireplace and picked up a heavy iron poker. "You coming, you stupid bird, or do you think you can explain your way out of this?" Without looking back, he followed Honus.

Rooster stood in the room, looking at the shattered vases - there were now six of them. And scattered and torn books. And scratched furniture. And the unconscious man. And, even though he couldn't see them from where he currently stood, several large dollops of droppings up on the shelves. "Maybe in a traditional publishing I could." He shook his head. "I need a better agent," he said as he left the room, closing the door behind him.

"Which way?" Honus said as he caught up to Gertie. "Do you know the way out?"

"Of course, I do," Gertie answered. "Weren't you paying attention as we were brought in?"

"We took so many turns and stairs, how was I supposed to remember?" Honus said. He looked at Marren. "Do you?"

Marren shook his head. "Nope. Follow the goat."

Gertie reached a staircase that led in both directions. "Okay. Okay."

"Do you remember or not?" Marren snapped.

"I do." Gertie answered. "Okay... we'll have to do it in reverse. That means it's up, then up again, then down, then down again. Then the first left, first right, then left and right again.

"What?" Honus asked. "How could you remember that?"

"It's as simple as getting from point B to A."

"Isn't that from A to B?" Marren said. He looked back as Rooster caught up.

Rooster was looking at the floor, sullen.

"Not when you're doing it backwards." Gertie gestured at the staircase. "So up one floor, across to the other stairwell then up again. Let's go."

With that, the quartet headed off.

~~~~~~~~~~~~~~~~~~~~~~~~~~~

The Witch of the East landed out of view of the castle. "Lousy, pompous, overbearing..." She got off her broom and held it to her side. "Blue wearing, soft, slug." She took a deep breath. "My room, my room, my room," she said as she clicked the heels of her ruby boots.

Within several seconds, she reappeared in her room.

The Witch did a quick spin in her room- it was empty. "Mirror, mirror on the wall!" she said, summoning the Djin.

The face reappeared almost immediately. "Back already? How'd it go?"

"She's responsible."

The face's eyes got large. "She admitted it?"

"Not in so many words, but it was her. I'm sure of it." She removed her cape and hung it on the chair in front of her vanity. "And news of our guests?"

"They were taken to the Zen Room. There are no mirrors there so that's all I know." He smirked. "You should have one added there."

206

"No privacy is everywhere in this place," the Witch said. "I'm not installing any more mirrors." She gestured at the curtains on either side of the mirror. "Even with curtains."

"Very well." The face said, obviously let down. As it was, his domain was limited to the mirrors in the castle, as well as two secretly installed mirrors- one with Witch of the West, and the other in the Grand Room of the Wizard himself. A third was going be installed by a paid-off traveling mirror salesman in the castle of the south later in the month.

"I'll let you know what's going on there. See if there is any news from the Wizard."

The face nodded. "And I guess I can check in on the Witch of the West." He grimaced. "I just wish they hadn't installed that mirror in her bathroom."

"It's better than nothing," said the Witch as she turned and left.

The Djin wasn't too sure.

~~~~~~~~~~~~~~~~~~~~~~~~

Taking the stairs - both up and down- two at a time, the Witch reached the Zen Room and skidded to a halt in front of the carved doors. She leaned forward and listened, hoping to garner some knowledge before entering the room occupied by an assassin and their associates.

She heard nothing.

She carefully pushed down on the handle and eased the door open. When it was wide enough, she started to poke her head in, then it occurred to her that it would make an easy target for a would-be assassin.

Taking several steps back, she charged the door instead, knocking it completely open as she entered. On her second step into the room, her foot slipped and she skidded in, wheeling her arms to keep her balance. Looking down, she saw numerous shards of pottery. The bright colors and patterns let her know they were Ozmanian Dynasty pottery. She bent down and picked up a piece. "What the?"

A groan made her turn and look. Her Valet was on his hands and knees, working his way to his feet. There was a puddle of blood under him.

"Ramone!" She exclaimed as she moved to the man. "What happened?"

"I'm not sure." The man shook his head, causing the room to spin. He sat back on his heels. "I think I was hit with a vase." He looked down at the blood intermixed with broken ceramic. "Most annoying." He looked at the Witch. "Are you okay?"

"I'm fine." She put her hand on the man's shoulder. "That is a pretty nasty gash. You need that looked at."

The man waved her off. "I'll be fine. We have interlopers in the castle that need dealt with."

"Assassins?"

"Buffoons, if I were to make a guess." He looked around the room. "There was an all-out brawl going on when got here."

The witch stood and offered her hand to the man. "What were they fighting over?"

The man let himself get pulled to his feet. "The rooster." He put his hands to the side of his head and winced.

"They were fighting over the rooster?"

"No, the rooster was the cause of the fight." The man startled. "The talisman. He was wearing the Snow Witch's talisman!"

He took a wobbly step toward the door. "We've got to stop them before they get out."

"I'll deal with that. You get to the infirmary and get your head looked at." She patted the man's shoulder. "No one attacks my Valet and gets away with it."

"Give them hell, Miss." Ramone said. He moved her hand and stood on his own. "I'll get to the nurses just fine."

"Meet you there." The Witch said. She jogged out of the room to the first intersection. There was a bell hanging from an ornate hook there. She took the wooden mallet and banged the bell three times- indicating that there were intruders within the castle. The sounds reverberated through the halls and up the stairs. After a moment, the sounds of other bells ringing let her know that the alarm was being passed throughout the castle. Within moments, outer windows and doors were being bolted and guarded. "Now I've got you." A smile played across her face. "And that talisman. We'll see what blue britches thinks of that."

~~~~~~~~~~~~~~~~~~~~~~~~~~

"What's that sound?" Honus said as they turned what he hoped was the last corner.

"If I had to guess, I'd say those were warning bells." Marren said. "We're in trouble."

"There it is." Gertie said as they rounded a corner- to the right. "The door we came in through."

"Nicely done, Gertie," Marren said.

Honus moved ahead of the group and put his shoulder against the door as he worked the handle. "I just hope there's no one outside waiting for us."

"Come ON!" Marren said. "We were so close, too!"

Rooster just kept quiet. It was difficult, but he managed.

Honus peered into the courtyard. "It's empty! Let's go."

"That's all I need, let's go Gertie!" Marren scooted around the goat and into the open area. An arrow seemed to appear in the ground next to him.

"That's weird," Honus said as he too stepped through the door. "Was that there a second ago?"

"Run for it!" Marren said as he sprinted for the portcullis. Which was coming down.

"Go, go, go!" Gertie exclaimed. "Hop on Rooster, we're getting out of here."

Rooster half hopped, half flapped to the goat's back, feet gripping her fur tightly. "On board." He said simply.

Gertie quickly overtook Marren and caught up to Honus who was surprisingly fast for a human. "Wow, you're quick."

"I've had a lot of practice," Honus said. "But really, I only need to be fast for about ninety feet."

"Ninety feet? Why?"

"That's the distance between the bases you're supposed to run from."

The pair ducked under the portcullis as it continued its downward track. "Hurry up, Marren!" Gertie called as she spun around.

"Why aren't you more like Dwarves?" Rooster called.

Gertie craned her neck to look at him. "What?"

"They're natural sprinters. Very dangerous over short distances." Rooster cocked his head to the side. "Of course."

The portcullis lowered completely, its spikes settling a full foot into the stone courtyard.

"Oh no!" Honus shook his head. "He's trapped!"

Marren continued to run at a full sprint.

"What's he doing?" Honus said. He took a step back.

"What's going on down there?" A guard called from the top of the gate. "We' re on lockdown you know!"

Marren finally reached the massive portcullis. He ducked his head and ran through the openings between the giant wood beams that formed the gate's defenses. "Sorry; that's as fast as I can run."

"I'm glad you are the size you are," Rooster said.

Marren looked at the bird. "Really?" He snapped.

Rooster nodded. "Yeah; otherwise we'd have lost you."

"Hey!" The soldier called down again. "Hey you two!"

Gertie looked up. "Huh."

"I'm officially offended," Rooster declared. "Highly and completely offended."

"Settle down, Rooster. Let's just get out of here." Honus said.

Marren winked at Rooster. "Watch this." He scooted out to where he could see the soldier. "Ho there!"

"What?" The soldier called down. "We're on lockdown; no one leaves!"

"They went thataway!" Marren pointed at the nearby treeline. "There were two of them and we're going to bring them back!"

"I'm not sure I believe..."

"Are you impugning the integrity of a Munchkin?" Roster called up at the man. "That's just plain rude!"

"Well I never meant..." The soldier stammered.

"They're getting away! Follow me!" Marren started for the trees.

Gertie and Honus exchanged glances. Then started running, making sure they didn't run faster than the Munchkin.

"Don't worry; we'll bring them back!" Rooster shouted. "I mean, if one can't trust a Munchkin, we've got bigger problems!"

The soldier waved. "Good luck! See you soon!"

"Who are you talking to now, Teddy?" Another soldier walked up to the man. "I know we've all talked to you about that."

"Hey there, Bill." Teddy pointed at the group that was almost to the trees by now. "They're going to get the invaders."

"What?"

"That helpful Munchkin said they were going to go get them and bring them back. The rooster even confirmed it." He smiled. "See?"

Bill flipped Teddy over the parapet toward the stone walkway almost fifty feet below "Idiot. The only thing worse than trusting a Munchkin, is trusting a rooster."

~~~~~~~~~~~~~~~~~~~~~~~~~~

Rooster watched as the guard cartwheeled off the top of the castle gates and landed with an audible crash. "Eeeesh." He said.

"What?" Gertie was looking forward as they ran. "What is it?"

"Nothing." Rooster said. "A changing of the guards, I think it's called."

The group stopped when they reached the trees.

Marren put his hands on his knees as he tried to catch his breath. He looked up at Rooster. "Thanks."

Rooster ruffled his feathers. "Don't mention it."

"Sure." Marren smiled. "Sure."

"No, really; do not mention it. Ever."

"Why?" Gertie asked.

"If word gets out that a rooster has gone soft, chickens stop listening to him and it's work, work, work all day long." He pointed at himself. "I don't need that kind of life."

Marren laughed. "Well, no one will hear it from me. In fact..."

A horn blew in the castle.

"And that's the 'keep running' horn, I think," Rooster said. He cocked his head at the Munchkin. "You ready? I'm not even tired yet."

"You're welcome," Gertie said.

"You got room up there for two?" Marren smirked.

The horn sounded again.

"Okay, we really need to get going," Honus said. He looked around. "Which way is it to the castle of that blue witch?"

"Are we still trying to get there?"

Honus started walking into the forest. "Yes! She's the only one that can get me home." He put his hand on the talisman. "With this."

"I don't know if we should trust her, Honus," Marren said as he fell in step beside him.

"I don't think we should either," Gertie said. "Rooster?"

"I don't trust anyone that isn't me." Rooster said.

"That's kind of narrow minded." Honus said.

"Keen, focused mind is more like it," Rooster corrected.

"So which way is her castle from here?" Honus asked.

"North, of course." Rooster said. He pointed East.

"Here we go again." Marren shook his head. "Just when I thought we were making some progress."

"I'm telling you." Rooster pointed again. "North is that way. Towards where the sun comes up."

"Gertie?"

Gertie nodded at Honus. "The castle is..." She glanced at Rooster. "More over in that direction than actually due North."

"How far?"

"Not more than a couple days' travel, I don't think." Gertie said. "As long as there are no detours."

"Why don't we just use the necklace to get us there?" Rooster asked. "Instead of just schlepping it for two days. My feet'll get blistered."

"You're riding on the goat!" Marren said. "You'll get blistered standing around for two days?"

"They'll get blistered when I pound on your head!"

"Everyone just calm down." Honus put his hand on the talisman. "Is... is there a way for this to get us to her castle right away?"

"It's powerful magic, Honus. Powerful." Marren said. "Using it without knowing what you're doing could be lethal."

"Really?"

"Do you know anything about magic? At all?"

Honus shook his head. "No. Not a thing. I didn't think it was even real before coming here. Wherever here is."

"Then just leave it to the professionals." Marren warned. "Using a powerful object like that isn't like waving a wand to make it rain."

"Wands can make it rain?"

"It's settled; we walk." Rooster said. He leaned to the side and stretched his foot out. "My poor feet." He leaned the other way and stretched the other leg. Then he sat down. "I'm ready."

"Let's get going then," Honus started walking. "Before those guards find us and we end up right back where we started."

"Before I saved you," Gertie said. "Right?"

"Absolutely." Marren said. He started walking as well. "So, two days of walking. You know at my size, that's like four days to scale."

"How do you figure?" Honus asked.

"For every one step you take, I take two. I'm walking twice as far."

Honus nodded. "I didn't consider that." He looked at Gertie. "You want to kick him off?"

"And what, carry Marren?" Gertie said. "He might be short, but he's on the stout side. Way on the stout side. Near the border of stout and fat."

"That hurts." Marren said. He patted his formidable belly. "But I accept your assessment. We Munchkins are indeed on the portly side."

"You're on the other side of the channel from port-ly." Rooster said. "Nice, huh? Even the timing was spot on, I think."

"And now we talk about something besides my weight."

"Two days of walking?" Rooster said. "Or four in your case."

"There really aren't any other options," Marren said. "Gertie?"

"There's a path that runs parallel to the yellow brick road that leads to the castle."

"Is it safe?"

"Quadling country? Not really. But there are worse places. We'll be close to the graveyard; the path skirts right by it."

"And that's the only way?"

"Wait!" Marren said. "Wait just a tick." He did a little jig.

"Uh oh; Marren skipped a groove," Rooster said. "Poor little fella."

"Oh no, I'm right on *track*." He laughed and did another quick jig.

"You're scaring me." Rooster said.

"Track! Get it?"

"No, sorry." Honus admitted.

"We take the track. Gertie, you know, right?"

"Oh!" Gertie nodded. "I sure do." She looked at Honus. "We can take the Great Gillikin Railway!"

216

"I'm up for a train ride," Rooster said.

"You'll just sit and sleep in the train instead of on Gertie's back. What's the difference?"

"Gertie doesn't have a club car."

"And it goes the whole way?" Marren asked.

"Well, the Gillikin Railway runs all through Gillikin country, but recently a spur was opened that runs south to near here. It follows the Gillikin River then heads south through the Kumbricia Mountains." Marren pointed west. "Another spur is being added that runs West, all the way to Winkie country, but that's not open yet."

"But this railway line is?" Honus asked hopefully.

"Well, it's not canon," Marren admitted, "but it's there."

"There's a cannon?" Honus said. "On the train?"

"Not exactly." Marren answered.

Rooster shook his head. "I'm telling you; first chance I get, I'm calling my agent. Simon and Schuster wouldn't pull this gimmick." He tilted his head to the side. "Penguin might. And they'd put a large breasted woman who has nothing to do with the plot on the cover."

"What about chicken breasts?" Marren suggested. "We got them, right?"

"I'm a rooster, in case you have forgotten. Folks don't eat roosters."

"I've always wondered about that," Honus said. "Why do you think that is?"

"Because we're majestic." Rooster said simply. "Chickens aren't."

"Huh." Honus said as he considered it. "Guess that's why cows are eaten regularly and horses aren't."

"Exactly." Rooster put his head back down. "Now you've got it."

"So how far to this train?" Honus asked.

Marren looked around to get his bearings. "If we head nor..." He glanced at Rooster then pointed. "That way for a couple of hours, we'll get to the tracks. They'll be running perpendicular to us so we can't miss them."

"Unless we end up in the cemetery." Gertie said.

"We'll know if we're going to far West if the ground gets swampy, then we can just angle East to make sure we don't go anywhere near it."

"What's so bad about a cemetery? It's just graves and stuff," Honus said.

"It's not the folks in the ground you have to worry about, kid," Marren said. "We keep away from that place no matter what."

Rooster tucked his head under his wing. "Let me know when we get there."

"So you can go to sleep?" Marren said. "Isn't that what you're doing now?"

"Right now, I'm napping. Later I'll be sleeping."

"Those are the same thing."

"If there were the same thing, why are they spelled differently?"

Marren opened his mouth then closed it. "Hmm." Was all he could manage.

"So an easy…" Honus started. A sharp look from Marren made him stop. Pointing at him with the iron poker helped as well. "We just walk that way with Gertie leading the way then." He nodded at Marren. "Better?"

"You're catching on." Marren replied with a smile.

The group walked in silence through the forest as the sun rose higher in the sky.

Except Rooster; he was ~~sleeping~~. Napping.

~~~~~~~~~~~~~~~~~~~~~~~~~~~

The Witch of the North took a sip of her tea.

A table and chair had been set up in her Scrying Chamber so she could monitor the progress of the Munchkin, the goat, and the young man. And occasionally she would peek in on the Witch of the West and giggle at her broom enchanting efforts.

Since leaving the castle, they had been heading in a generally northward direction. She had assumed they were going to walk the entire two-day distance so she had wandered off, planning on checking on their progress occasionally.

It wasn't until an hour later, when the grey bubbles of a train made her realize they were walking toward the newly installed, non-canon rail line. With about thirty minutes to spare, she had sent a bubble to the Gillikin main train station and coordinated for a smaller train to pass by where the group would cross the tracks.

She took a bite of her scone. "Excellent. This will get them here by dinner time." The witch put her feet up on the railing. "And my plan comes together nicely." She resisted steepling her fingers and tapping them together and instead took another bite of her scone. "On the tracks of inevitability. She allowed herself just one evil chuckle: "Mwa hah hah!" Before taking a sip of her Ozjeeling Tea. "Ahhh."

~~~~~~~~~~~~~~~~~~~~~~~~~~~

After a little more than two hours, the group reached a raised railroad track. Sitting on it was a brightly colored locomotive and matching coal car. There was one passenger car attached to the coal car with a bright red caboose at the end to finish off the tiny train.

"Well, that is an unusual sight," Honus said. "What's it doing sitting out here in the middle of nowhere?"

"There is no way it is here by accident," Marren said.

"I agree."

Marren put his hand on Gertie's shoulder. "Then it's unanimous; we keep walking and avoid the obvious trap."

The engineer leaned out from the locomotive and waved. "Hey ho!"

"A train? What luck!" Rooster said "Ahoy!" He waved back.

"That's for boats, I think," Honus said.

"Helloooo!" Rooster said without missing a beat.

"Hey ho!" The engineer said again as he waved. Again.

"There is no way we should get on that train," Marren said.

"Nowww boarding!" A conductor shouted as he leaned out from the front of the passenger car.

"What luck!" Rooster hopped off Gertie and ran toward the train.

"Stop you stupid bird!" Honus took several steps toward the train.

"Rooster!" Marren called.

Rooster skidded to a stop beside the conductor. "Good day to you sir!"

"Good day, noble rooster."

"Rooster come back!" Marren shouted.

Rooster patted his sides. "It seems I'm a little light on funds. Can you extend some credit our way?"

The conductor laughed. "Why, my fine feathered friend, there is no money in Oz! Everyone shares equally and gives with kindness to others in need." He gestured up the stairs. "So in you go."

Rooster cocked his head. "No money because everyone gives freely and lives equally?"

"That is the way it is." The conductor assured with a smile. "Of course."

Rooster gestured behind him. "Then why is there only one huge castle back there and with a bunch of drafty, thatch covered shacks around it, instead of a bunch of castles, or only thatch covered shacks?

The conductor's smile faltered slightly.

"But as you said, everyone is created equal."

"Yes!" The man's smile returned.

"But some are more equal than others."

The man's smile faltered again.

Rooster looked down at his feet. "Where are you in the whole 'four legs good, two legs bad' debate? We birds got the short end of the stick on that one, I think."

"On you go," the conductor said flatly. He gestured up the stairs.

"So you're telling me folks give freely to one person to have a castle while they live in a hovel, while others freely work in said castle as serv... ACK!"

The conductor grabbed Rooster by the neck and tossed him up the stairs. He looked at the group- they were all staring at him.

"Now. Boarding." He said sternly. He leaned out from the bottom step, holding onto a polished brass handle at arm's length. The other arm just hung loosely, swinging back and forth. He looked to the front of the train then the back. Then he started staring at Honus, Marren, and Gertie.

"I think we need to do what he says." Honus said.

"Let's just let them take Rooster. If they are bad guys, they deserve each other." Marren said.

"Hey ho!" The engineer said.

Everyone turned to look at him.

The engineer smiled wide. And raised the loaded crossbow up to his cheek. He never lost his smile.

"Well then." Marren said. "I guess we're riding." He gestured. "After you, ma'am."

Gertie started toward the train. "At least we're not walking to our doom."

The engineer took his front hand off the cross bow and waved to her. "Hey ho, goat!" he said. Then he went back to aiming at her as she walked. Once she was aboard, he swiveled the crossbow around and aimed toward Marren and Honus.

Marren put his hand on Honus' back and pulled him along as he also started toward the train. "Sit opposite me at the other end of the train."

"Why?"

"It will make it harder for them to kill us all at once and whichever of us isn't killed will have a chance to do something."

"Oh." He looked down at the man. "You have... experience with this?"

"Maybe a little." Marren said noncommittally. No matter what, he wanted his 'no convictions' record to continue. He nodded at the conductor. "Can we get a ride, good sir?"

"Most assuredly, my good and noble Munchkin." The conductor pulled himself upright as he gestured up the steps. "In fact, I believe that lunch is to be served as soon as we are on our way, so your timing is impeccable."

Marren looked at Honus. "First they kill you with kindness."

"Then what?"

Marren shrugged as he started up the stairs. "Then they just kill you."

"Welcome aboard, young man," the conductor said. He gestured up the steps again.

"Who do you work for?" Honus moved to the first step so they were eye to eye.

"The railway of course." The man smiled.

"I mean really."

The man's smile disappeared.

The two stared at each other for a full ten seconds.

The man leaned out and looked forward then back, then forward again. "Allll 'boarrrd!"

The engineer's head disappeared back into the locomotive and the whistle sounded two short toots.

"Get to your seat, young man. We're going to shovel the coal and let this rattler roll." He put his hand on Honus' back and shoved him up the stairs. "Why don't you have a seat right next to your Munchkin friend." He didn't say it as a question.

With numb legs, Honus walked up the remaining three steps and turned right into the passenger car. It was as brightly colored on the inside as it was on the outside, except instead of paint, it had received a liberal application of bright velour and leather. And crystal chandeliers and sconces. Marren was sitting on the far side of the passenger car. Gertie was on the floor in the open area between where the one set of seats faced forward and the other backward. Honus walked over and sat beside Marren. "They're going to kill us."

"So let's not make it easy for them, huh?" Marren hopped off his plush seat and walked to the far end of the car on the opposite side of Honus and climbed onto the equally plush seat. He winked at Honus. "Good luck and duck."

Rooster entered the passenger car from the rear door. "This is traveling in style." He gestured over his shoulder. "The caboose is nicer than this one, if you can imagine." He perked up. "Ahh, Jeeves."

Marren turned to look.

The conductor gave a nod. "Master Rooster. How goes the tour?"

"Excellent, Jeeves. Excell..."

The train lurched as it started to move.

"Ahh," Rooster said. "Know what that means?"

"We're moving?" Honus tried.

"Our time is almost up?" Marren offered.

"Lunch is served," Jeeves and Rooster said at the same time.

Marren mouthed 'poison' to Honus then ran a finger across his throat.

"We're not hungry, sir," Honus said.

"What?" Rooster exclaimed. "Not hungry? Ohhh. Right; they're *starving*. Bring on the grub, Jeeves." He cocked his head to the side. "For me at least, these fellows will take human food, of course. An old can and some newspaper would be enough for the goat."

"I swear," Gertie swore.

"We're fine, Sir," Honus said.

Jeeves smiled. "Ahhh. You are worried about the food. If it will help, I can eat some of it before you do." He gave a short bow. "I can assure you that you are not to be poisoned."

"Then how will we die?" Marren asked.

Jeeves considered that for a moment. "Well, my good Munchkin, I truly hope you all die of extreme old age." With that he walked through the car and into the caboose.

"And why are you insulting our host?" Rooster snapped.

"Because there is no reason this train should be out here in the middle of nowhere!" Gertie said. "All ready to go, waiting for us."

"Well... maybe the Witch of the North was keeping an eye on our progress and decided to send us some help since we are on our way back to her. Did you consider that?" Rooster said.

"No, I didn't." Honus said honestly.

"Well, since this train runs north," Rooster pointed east. "It will take us right to her castle."

"Oh boy." Marren said. "Listen, I say we subdue this one and find out what he knows."

"What?" Rooster did a little hop. "Before our meal is served? That's... that's... that's just plain rude is what that is."

"Listen, Rooster," Honus began. He stopped when the rear door of the car opened and Jeeves came in pushing a cart.

"Why don't we just ask him?" Rooster said.

"Because it has been my experience that folks that are looking to cause you harm also have no issue lying to you about it. Or anything else for that matter!" Marren said.

"Is there a problem?" Jeeves asked. He stopped in the middle of the car and looked at Gertie. "You will be pleased to know I did not bring any empty cans for you, Miss Goat."

"That's nice of you." Gertie said, still not convinced with the man's honesty. "What'd I get?"

Jeeves looked down at the cart. "Let's see, shall we?" He lifted a large silver top releasing a cloud of steam. "Seems we have noodles and mussels in a light marinara sauce here." He put the lid back in place and lifted another one. "A large salad with a vinaigrette dressing to share here." He moved to the last platter and lifted that lid. "And in the last one, some Turkish Delight for dessert." He held both lids out with his arms extended. "How does that sound?"

"Actually, that sounds nice." Gertie looked at Marren. "To be honest with you."

"That's always a good policy."

"What is the plan, Jeeves?" Marren asked as he hopped off the seat. He was still holding the iron poker.

"You mean after the meal?"

"In general."

Jeeves returned the lids to their respective platters. "We have a three-and-a-half-hour trip ahead of us so I imagine it will go like this." He put his hands behind his back. "First you will eat lunch, then some of you will nap."

"That's me," Rooster interrupted.

"Others will enjoy the sights and perhaps search the car." He took a step towards the rear of the car. "Then after about two and a half hours, I will serve a light snack and refreshments."

"I'll be awake for that, Jeeves," Rooster assured. "I assure you."

"Excellent," Jeeves said. "Then an hour after that, we will arrive at the castle of the Witch of the North. Where you will be taken to one of her many fine rooms, exchange pleasantries, finish whatever dealings you have, then make a hasty departure. By then, this train will be at another station picking up other patrons to take them to their destination."

"And the part where we get killed?"

Jeeves smiled at Honus. "That, my young man, is between you and the witch. If you want my opinion, I think that once she gets the talisman of the Witch of the South, you will be so inconsequential to her that she won't even acknowledge your presence without you making a real effort to get her attention. At best."

"And a worst case?" Honus asked.

"At worst, she'll have you tossed out on your rear ends."

"And we're supposed to believe you why?" Marren asked.

"Because it's the truth?" Jeeves said. "Do you want me to sample each dish before I leave? Because I will if you ask me."

"That's fine, Jeeves," Rooster said. "And I have to say that I apologize for the way these others are acting. Rude is what they are being. Right in the face of your gracious hospitality that is typical of riding the rails, I might add. A gentleman's way of travel, the railways. Trains truly are a place going somewhere."

Jeeves smiled sincerely. "I do appreciate that."

Honus looked at the floor. "Well, I suppose I'm sorry."

Marren put the poker on the seat. "Yeah, me too."

"Great, apologies all around! Now let's eat." Rooster said. "Thanks Jeeves."

"It is my pleasure." Jeeves gave another short bow and left for the caboose.

"I am hungry," Gertie said. "Now that it was mentioned." She got up and walked to the cart. "And it does smell good."

"It does, doesn't it?" Rooster said. "Honus, serve up what is probably the best lunch we've had in a week."

Honus smiled. "I suppose it is." He walked to the cart and took a plate from the shelf below the food. "Noodles and mussels, Gertie?"

"Sure. I'll skip the salad, I think."

With that the group ate what was definitely the best meal any of them had eaten in a week.

~~~~~~~~~~~~~~~~~~~~~~~~~

"Wake up."

Honus stirred.

"Wake up."

Someone slapped him.

"Wake up!"

Honus opened his eyes. His vision was blurry which made what he did see even more confusing. "Whuh?"

Honus was slapped again. Much, much harder this time.

"Wake! Up!"

Honus blinked, trying to get his eyes to focus. When they finally did, he was still confused- he felt like he was flat on his back and was looking at the upsidedown face of a woman.

"Finally."

The woman moved out of Honus' line of sight. He tried to turn his head, but it seemed to be tied in place.

He heard someone being slapped. It was followed by 'wake up'. Whoever was on the receiving end of the slap seemed to wake up after the first one because a second one wasn't administered.

The woman's face came into view again. "You still with me?"

"Where am I?"

Honus felt himself being lifted up. When he got to an upright position, the thing he was apparently tied to spun in a complete circle. He caught sight of Gertie in a small cage on the far side of the grey walled room.

The face of the Witch of the North came into view. "Welcome, weary traveler."

"Oh, hello," Honus said. He tried to move his arms. He couldn't, realizing he was tied to a large wooden wheel. "Why am I tied to this wheel?"

"Do you have the..."

"Oh, I am going to *kill* that stupid rooster," Marren said from somewhere else in the room.

The witch looked to her left. "Munchkin, if you interrupt me again, that bird will be the *least* of your troubles." She looked at Honus. "Do you have the pendant?"

Honus shifted his eyes around. "Pendant, what pendant?"

The witch nodded.

The wheel Honus was strapped to suddenly spun several times. Whoever was behind it stopped it with him upright and facing the witch again.

She smiled. "Do you have the pendant?"

"Yes." Honus said simply. A thought occurred to him. "But..."

"But?"

"But why didn't you just take it while we were knocked out?"

"I have my reasons."

"Well, Miss Witch, why don't you just take it and let us go?"

The witch reached out for the talisman, which was now hanging outside Honus' shirt. Sparks flew from it. She flinched back as she was shocked. "Fool! It can't be that easy."

"I'm sorry." Honus said. "Can we still go?"

"NO!"

"Hey," Marren called. "Esteemed Blue Witch of the North."

"What?!"

"How about we make a deal?"

The Witch turned to look at him. "What sort of deal?"

"How about we give you the star pendant and you let us go? I know it will come off Honus because I had it for a while and even Rooster wore it for a while. I think it's a matter of how one receives it."

The witch stepped back so both men could see her at once. "So, you'd be willing to give me the talisman?"

"For our release? Yes." Marren said.

"Put me down!" Rooster said as a soldier entered the room carrying him. "You don't know who you're dealing with!"

The guard walked up to the witch. "Sorry for the delay." He looked at Rooster. "There were complications."

"I'll show you a complication!" Rooster said. He tried to reach up and peck the man's hands. He was now wearing heavy leather gloves so he didn't let go of Rooster's legs. This time.

"Put him in a pot." The Witch said. "We'll have chicken and dumplings for dinner."

Rooster craned his head around to look at the Witch. "But I'm a rooster. One shouldn't meddle with a tried and true recipe like chicken and dumplings."

"I'll risk it." The Witch waved a hand, dismissing the soldier.

"Maybe we can stay for dinner," Marren said. "We'd finally get something useful out of that bird."

"I'll show you something useful!" Rooster said as he thrashed about.

231

"It would be a first!"

"First I'm going to fatten your lip!"

"Shut up!" The Witch shouted. She whirled around and stalked to the far wall. Several rows of weapons were displayed on a large rack there. She chose a long silver pole then turned back around. "The next one that speaks out of turn is going to get a sound thrashing."

Even Rooster stopped moving, though he still kept an eye on the Witch.

"Honus, give me the talisman." The Witch approached him.

"I will give it to you on two conditions," Honus said.

The Witch smiled. "And those are?"

"First, you let us all go. Me, Marren, Gertie, and Rooster."

"I can do that. And?"

"And you send me back home."

The Witch sighed. "I hear that there is no place like home."

Honus shrugged. "Well, home isn't all it's cracked up to be, but it's better than here. And will let me get on with my life."

"Don't trust her," Gertie said. Since she was in a cage and farthest from the Witch, she felt she had the best chance of not getting thrashed. "She'll just tell you what you want to hear."

Honus eyed the Witch. "That is true. How can we be sure that you will do what you promise?"

The Witch leaned on the pole. "I guess you'll just have to trust me." She said with a smirk.

"May I make a suggestion?" Rooster said.

"Quiet, Rooster," Gertie snapped.

232

"Oh, here we go," Marren said. "Your suggestions got us in this predicament in the first place."

"I know how to solve this problem, unlike you," Rooster said.

"Maybe we should listen to him," Honus said.

"Because it worked every other time?"

"With me as your leader, we were triumphant," Rooster declared.

"I don't see how you made it anywhere." The Witch said. "Honestly."

"Honus," Rooster said. "I know how to fix this. Trust me."

Marren snorted.

Honus looked from the Witch to Rooster and back. He couldn't turn his head to see Marren. "Okay, what do you suggest, Rooster?"

"First, you release us." Rooster said.

"I'm not letting you go just like that," the Witch said.

"No, not let us go, let us go; I mean untie them, let Gertie out of the cage, and put me on the ground, let us go. It's not like we'll be able to make a run for it from this dungeon." The rooster cocked his head to the side. "Then we can talk like adults." He hesitated for the smallest moment. "Even though one of us stopped growing when they were eight."

"I'm going to kick you into next week!" Marren said. "You won't even know what day it is, you stupid bird!"

"Marren, just calm down." Honus said.

"Yeah, calm your little head before it pops off your little body," Rooster snapped.

233

"SHUT UP!" The Witch banged the pole onto the stone floor. She tuned to Gertie. "How did you put up with this?"

"I chewed my cud loudly." Gertie admitted. "And I hummed a lot."

"That was you?" Rooster said. "I thought I had developed tinnitus."

"What's that?" Marren said.

"Something big people get," Rooster deadpanned. "That's why you've never heard of it."

"Oh, you're going to get it!" Marren thrashed against his bonds.

"I swear I'm going to beat you all senseless..." The Witch caught herself. "Not that any of you seem to have any sense anyway." She gestured at Gertie. "Except for her."

"Thanks."

"So if I untie you, you all better just keep to yourselves."

"Okay." Gertie said.

No one else said anything.

"*So if I untie you, you all better just keep to yourselves.*" The Witch seethed. She hit the silver pole onto the stone floor with a resounding 'clang'.

"Deal." Marren said.

"Fine by me," Rooster agreed.

"Release their bindings." The Witch commanded.

In short order, the group was standing on their own in the dungeon. But not next to each other.

"Okay Rooster," Honus said. "What do you suggest?"

Rooster strutted forward, directly in front of the Witch. He took several deep breaths.

"Well?" The Witch narrowed her eyes at the bird, expecting a simple demand that could easily -and legally- be interpreted however she liked.

Rooster took another very deep breath then said quickly: "Esteemed Witch of the North, do you now swear on your Coven that once you are in possession of the star talisman previously owned by the Witch of the South, that you will allow us to leave your castle unharmed and never hold any grudge against us which would cause you to take any personal action or order any action against any of us and furthermore return Honus to his home country and not hold any grudge against him eitherrrr?" His eyes were bulging out when he got to the end.

The Witch stared at Rooster.

"That was, I think, the longest run-on sentence I've ever heard." Marren said.

Not seeing any loopholes in what the bird had said- not even a pause that would signify a period and therefore a separate request that could just be ignored once the first was granted. "I swear on my Coven." She said sourly. She held out her hand.

"Hand it over, Honus; we're in the clear." Rooster said. He strutted back and forth. "And *that's* why I'm in charge."

Honus looked to Marren. "Yes?"

"I hate to say it, but it seems legitimate to me."

Honus removed the talisman from around his neck and held it out by the chain.

The Witch reached for the star then caught herself. Instead she took it by the chain and held it at arm's length. She looked around then to the silver rod she was holding. Carefully, she fed the chain into the hollow rod. When it was completely in, she held the rod upright so the star was balanced on the top. Again, without touching the star, she grasped the rod at its very top.

Hold fast and true

She incanted.

The top of the rod sealed around the chain, securing the star to it. "Finally!" She said as she hit the rod on the stones again.

It sounded as if a lightning bolt had struck in the room.

Everyone ducked.

Including the Witch.

"Geeze, lady!" Rooster said. "Take it easy with that thing!"

The smell of ozone lingered in the air.

"Open that door," the Witch said. "And a window." She held her nose as she gazed at the star. "Wow."

"Well, Witchie Poo," Rooster strutted over to Honus, "we'd love to stay, but... actually we all hate being here and want to leave."

"Rooster," Honus said, "you shouldn't say things like that."

"Pah," Rooster said. "We have a binding agreement that she has to follow."

"But that's no reason to be rude," Honus said.

The Witch shook her head. "You do need to go away, you won't last a week here." She pointed at the door. "Get out. All of you."

"Uhm, this might not be the best time to ask," Gertie said, "but have you had a chance to read my resume? Gertie, the chef?"

The Witch looked down at Gertie. "Are you Gertie, the famous chef?"

Gertie nodded. "That's me."

"And you're associating with... with... this lot?"

"They're not so bad once you get the hang of it. And you hum a lot."

"I am in the market for a chef." The Witch admitted. "And after meeting... them, I don't think I'll bother with even asking for references."

"Deal with what you're dealt." Gertie replied. "When life gives you dolts, make dolt-ade."

"We can hear you talking, you know." Rooster said.

Because they could.

"You're hired." The Witch said. She pointed at the door with her newly created wand. "The rest of you, get out."

Honus' eyes got large. "Leave?"

The Witch pointed the long wand at Honus. "Ready?"

Honus looked at Marren, then Gertie, then Rooster. "Right now?"

"I've got things to do." The Witch said. "It's now or never."

Honus went to Marren and extended his hand. "Thanks for everything Marren, I'll never forget you."

"Remember what we talked about," Marren said, "do what makes you happy, Walter."

"Walter?" Gertie said. "Walter is it?"

"Marren'll explain," Honus said. He moved to Gertie and got on his knees so he could hug her around her neck. "I'm going to miss you as well, Gertie. Thanks for everything."

"I'll miss you too... Walter."

Honus stood and turned to face Rooster.

"Don't get all mushy on me." Rooster said.

"See you around, Rooster," Honus said with a smile. He turned to the Witch. "Okay, I'm ready."

"Finally." The Witch exhaled loudly then pointed the four-foot-long wand at him. "Ready?"

"Yes." Honus smiled. "And I suppose I should thank you as...."

Be Gone!

The Witch incanted.

In a flash, Honus was in fact, gone.

"Finally." The Witch said. She pointed at the door. "Now you two imbeciles- get out."

"She just called you a double imbecile, Marren. Did you hear that?" Rooster said.

Marren shook his head. "See you later, Gertie." He waved and walked out of the room.

Rooster looked at the Witch. "Some folks." He said as he shook his head. "Right, Blues?"

The Witch nodded. At her soldier.

"I'm glad you agree with... ACK!"

The guard reached down and grabbed Rooster by the neck. "Word is that roosters are poor fliers but fair gliders."

"Works for me."

"Urk!" Rooster said.

The guard marched over to the window and pushed open the heavy wooden shutter. "Off you go." He said as he pitched Rooster out the window.

Rooster twisted in the air to get his feet under him. As he fell he spread his wings out wide. His fall immediately slowed and he started to glide away from the castle tower. "Like an eagle, I soar!" He shouted as he gracefully glided toward the ground. "Wait till I tell Marren!"

Chapter 4 - Kansas

"Wake up."

Honus stirred.

"Wake up."

Someone grabbed Honus' foot.

"Wake up!"

Honus startled awake. It was dark around him and when he tried to sit up, he banged his head- it seemed he was in a narrow space. "Where am I?"

"Honus, are you okay?" Staples asked.

"Where am I?"

"You're in the chicken coop!" Staples grabbed Honus' leg. "I can't pull you out. Are you stuck?"

Honus tried to move his arms and legs- they all worked. "No, I don't think so. Let me try sliding out."

"Sure thing!" Staples backed out of the chicken coop on all fours.

Within a few moments, Honus slid out on his back, feet first.

"Are you a sight for sore eyes!" Staples exclaimed. "We was worried you were a goner. I was especially, when you went for the coop instead of the basement."

"Where am I?" Honus sat up and rubbed his head. Then his elbow.

"You're in the chicken coop, hiding from the tornado." Staples pointed up at the dark sky- clouds were churning about as flashes of lightning lit them to striking shades of grey and deep blues. "Remember?"

"In Kansas?"

"Yeah." Staples chuckled. "You're at chicken coop, Kansas. The corner of lightning and tornadoes." He poked his friend on the shoulder. "Just like you said this morning. Those weathermen sure know their stuff."

"How long have I been here?" Honus rubbed his head.

Staples thought for a moment. "Half hour, I think."

"Half? Half an hour? But it's been days!"

"Days from what?"

"Days since I left... here."

"Listen," Staples said, "I think you've been hit on the head or somethin'. The tornado only went by a half hour ago." He gestured behind him. "Believe me, we were all payin' attention when it happened!"

"But, Rooster and Marren. And the witches." He rubbed his head.

"Witches?" Honus sat back on his heels. "You seen witches?"

Honus looked around. "I don't know. Maybe?"

"What'd they tell you? These witches?"

"I should follow my dreams or I would regret it."

"The witches told you that? Wow, that's... that's..."

"It wasn't a witch; it was this man I met. A really nice man who helped me. He saved my life even." He smiled. "He was a midget plumber."

"A midget plumber. A midget plumber gave you advice? Where was this?"

Honus looked up. "It's hard to say. It was a... magical place."

"Doesn't sound like Kansas." Interjected Staples.

"It was full of color. Bright and cheery."

"Definitely not Kansas."

"And strange people."

"Well, that could be Kansas." Staples smiled. "It's good you're home now, right? Safe and sound?"

Honus worked to his feet. He rubbed his arm where he had banged it. "Oh, I'm not staying here."

"Pittsburg?"

"Pittsburg. I'm going to play baseball, not hang around here. I know in my heart I can be great at it."

"If that's what you gotta do, then that's what you gotta do." Staples said. "When you leavin'?"

Honus extended his hand to his friend. "Tonight. Once I get my stuff."

Staples took his friend's hand and allowed himself to be pulled to his feet. "Well, we'll give you a good send off, that's for sure."

Honus shook his head. "No, I think I just want to leave nice and quiet like. Not cause a ruckus. You know?"

Staples nodded. "Yeah." He smiled. "Wish I could have seen the place."

Something someone else told him popped into his head. "Well, if I understand right, if the reviews are good, maybe you will."

242

"Reviews? What reviews? Who told you that; that plumber?"

"It was one of the witches."

"Yeah, sure." Staples said. "You're just pulling my leg now."

Honus put his arm over his friend's shoulder as they started for the front of the house. "You're a good friend, Staples. If you're ever in Pittsburg, you should come for a visit."

"Sure Honus.

"Walter."

"What?"

"My real name is Walter Johnson." Walter said with a smile. "That way you'll know who to look for. "You won't find me as Barney and I'm pretty sure Honus Wagner won't be interested in visiting with you."

"Walter Johnson. What do you think about that." Staples said. "Well, I'll definitely look you up." He nudged his friend. "Won't be hard to find since you're going to be a famous baseball player and all. Right?"

"Nope." Walter said.

"Nope."

The pair rounded the corner of the house and headed to the front door.

The End

(Unless the reviews are good. Then Staples is going on a trip.)

~~~~~~~~~~~~~~~~~~~~~~~

(Epilogue)

The Witch of the West leaned back in her room-wide tub. It was for all intents and purposes, an indoor pool. A large one.

"Ahhh." She said. As she squirted water out of her hands, making little fountains. "This is nice."

Marren surfaced near the far side of the bath. "Made it almost the whole way!"

"Very nice," The Witch said absently. "Very nice indeed."

Marren chuckled. "You aren't talking about me, are you."

The Witch looked over at the Munchkin. "Oh, well... very impressive. But I was commenting on the events of the past couple of weeks."

"It has been eventful." Marren back-stroked across the bath to her. "All's well that ends well." He sat on a ledge near the Witch. "I'm sorry about losing the talisman," he added. "She has it on a silver pole and it never leaves her side."

The Witch nodded. "It's okay, dear. We'll get it."

"At least you have the shoes. It's a good thing she tossed them instead of using them against you."

The Witch shook her head. "There's no way she ever would."

Marren looked up at her. "Really?"

"Guaranteed. There is no way that blue-loving Witch was ever going to put on a pair of clashing ruby shoes. No matter how powerful they were."

"What about you?"

"I'll wear an extra-long skirt. And maybe a ruby sash."

"A sash would be nice." Marren said. "And maybe some bright red lipstick. We still need a way to get that talisman, though." Marren said. "That'll be nearly impossible."

"With the Witch of the South gone and my poor sister killed by that maniacal girl..." She sat up. "What is it with people from that place- Kansas? They're homicidal lunatics!" She leaned back again. "At least that blue idiot in the North thinks I'm dead." She squirted more water out of her hands. "She won't expect it at all when I show up. Talisman or not, I've got my broom and the shoes." She smiled at him. "She won't know what hit her. Especially with that fool the wizard gone." She put her arm around Marren. "You'll see."

Marren leaned his head against her breast. "Yes, dearest." He sighed contentedly.

About the Author

I'm still retired and still writing. And spending a lot of time messing around with my Jeep Wrangler, which is fun. So is the writing. Mainly because it lets me surf the internet for a wild assortment of facts- such as baseball players from the 1900's. Or 'can chickens fart.' and "how do poisons work'. If the FBI ever seizes my computer and looks at my searches, I might end up in a SuperMax. Or more likely, a loony bin.

The idea for this story came about one sunny day while I was out with my long-suffering wife wandering around Disney's Hollywood Studios. Wanting to get out of the sun for a while, and seeing a ten-minute wait, we decided to ride the (air conditioned!) Great Movie Ride. It's not there anymore, so if you haven't ridden it, you're out of luck unless you can find a YouTube video of it. It's a fun ride through classic movie scenes with audio animatronics as well as a couple of live actors and a cheesy classic-Disney twist in it. BUT -at one point you ride through the set of Wizard of Oz where Dorothy and the Blue Witch are chatting when the Witch of the West shows up in town.

When we did it- the ride stopped. So we sat. And sat. And sat. Listening to the Munchkins sing about following the Yellow Brick Road. For about five or six minutes. While we sat, I looked over at Dorothy and the Blue Witch and noticed that the Yellow Brick Road only seemed to spiral out because there was also a Red Brick Road spiraling out. 'I wonder where that road goes?' I thought as the Munchkins sang. Over and over.

Truly and honestly, I had no idea this theme had even been discussed until about three quarters of the story was written-which is when I start working on my cover. This is for two reasons-

First- I like the cover of my stories to have something to do with the plot. A lot of pulp fiction books have really cool ships on the cover, and/or a scantily clad female of some species or another that have nothing to do with the story inside. So I like to wait until later on to start on it. Second, and more importantly, when I get my artists and cover designers working on it, that gives me a self-imposed two-week deadline to have the first draft of the story done; when the cover will be finished.

So that's when I actually did a search for "Wizard of Oz Red Brick Road" to see if I could get a better image of the road than the one I took on the Great Movie Ride to pass to my illustrator. And heaps of hits popped up. There were lots of images, several sites discussing the road's destination, fan fiction, and even a cancelled television series! I then spent the rest of the afternoon reading through the sites. Some of it was fun. Some of it shocking. There was definitely a lot to read but since I was three quarters through with the book and had sent 'Hey, are you still alive?' emails to my artist and cover designer, the two-week deadline had been set. So, I got back to writing.

Unlike some of the really, really dark stuff I read online (promiscuous Dorothy and crucified Flying Monkeys- really??), I like to think that I kept with the whimsical style of the Oz series. Yes, there's a lot of satire, and for the first time in any of my writing, I broke the 'fourth wall'. Or maybe it's the 'fourth page' when it's written. If you hear that term anywhere else later on, I coined it here and now as I write at 1230AM. If you read my *Tales From a Second Hand Wand Shop* series next, I'm sorry to say you've already read a couple of the jokes here that I used in that series as well. There are definitely similarities between Rooster and Grimbledung. Of course, being a Gnome, Grimbledung can fart, so you get more fart jokes in that series. You're welcome.

Oh- I never could come up with a good crack about apes for Rooster, sorry.

For what it's worth- Walter Johnson had an illustrious career in baseball, including holding the record for most strikeouts (3,508) that stood until Nolan Ryan broke it 55 years later in 1983. He is known as one of the "Immortal Five"- who along with Ty Cobb, Christy Mathewson, Babe Ruth, and Honus Wagner was among first five players inducted into the Baseball Hall of Fame.

President Calvin Coolidge shakes Walter Johnson's hand!

He was an upstanding and honest fellow and a tribute to baseball. I'm pretty sure he never got along with roosters though.